HOPEFUL

Center Point
Large Print

Also by Shelley Shepard Gray and available
from Center Point Large Print:

The Days of Redemption Series
  Daybreak
  Ray of Light

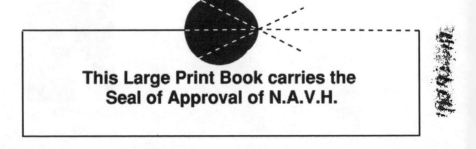

HOPEFUL

Return to Sugarcreek Series
— Book One —

SHELLEY SHEPARD GRAY

CENTER POINT LARGE PRINT
THORNDIKE, MAINE

This Center Point Large Print edition is published in the year 2014 by arrangement with Avon Inspire, an imprint of HarperCollins Publishers.

Copyright © 2014 by Shelley Shepard Gray.

"Fanny Kay's Chocolate Cream Pie" recipe from *Simply Delicious Amish Cooking* by Sherry Gore (Zondervan, 2012) reprinted with permission.

The text of this Large Print edition is unabridged. In other aspects, this book may vary from the original edition. Printed in the United States of America on permanent paper. Set in 16-point Times New Roman type.

ISBN: 978-1-62899-046-1

Library of Congress Cataloging-in-Publication Data

Gray, Shelley Shepard.
Hopeful / Shelley Shepard Gray. — Center Point Large Print edition.
pages ; cm
ISBN 978-1-62899-046-1 (library binding : alk. paper)
1. Restaurateurs—Fiction. 2. Infatuation—Fiction.
    3. Large type books. I. Title.
PS3607.R3966H67 2014b
813'.6—dc23
                                                                2013040996

To anyone who has ever volunteered
to help someone learn to read.
I hope you found, like I did,
that it was time well spent.

Having hope will give you courage.
JOB 11:18

⌇

It is far more important to be the right person
than to find the right person.
AMISH PROVERB

Chapter One ✟

September

She was late.

Holding her canvas tote bag in one hand and a box of oatmeal-raisin cookies in the other, Miriam Zehr exited her house, darted down her street, turned left on Main Street, and almost ran down old Mr. Sommers.

With a grunt, he stepped to the side, his garden hose spraying a good bit of water onto her skirts before settling back onto his daffodils.

She skidded to a stop. "I'm sorry, Eli."

He merely raised one eyebrow. "Late again, Miriam?"

"*Jah.*" As discreetly as possible, she shook her blue apron and dress a bit. A few drops flew from the fabric, glinting in the morning sun.

He shook his head in exasperation. "One day you're going to injure someone with your haste."

She winced. "I know. And I am sorry, Eli."

Looking at the box in her hand, his voice turned wheedling. "Those cookies?"

"They're oatmeal-raisin." When his eyes brightened, she set down her tote and carefully opened the box. "Care for one?"

After setting the hose down, he reached in and

pulled out two plump cookies. "Girl who cooks as *gut* as you should be married by now."

She'd heard the same refrain almost as often as she'd run late for work. "I've often thought the same thing," she said as she picked up her tote again. "But for now, I must be on my way."

"Have a care, now." He shook one arthritic finger at her. "Not everyone's as spry as me, you know."

"I'll be careful," she promised before continuing on her way to work.

Once at the Sugarcreek Inn, she would put on a crisp white apron. Then, she'd divide her time between baking pies and serving the restaurant's guests. The whole time, she'd do her best to smile brightly. Chat with customers and her coworkers. And pretend she didn't yearn for a different life.

But first, she had to get to work on time.

"Going pretty fast today, Miriam," Joshua Graber called out from the front porch of his family's store. "How late are you?"

"Only five minutes. Hopefully."

He laughed. "Good luck. Stop by soon, wouldja? Gretta would love to see you."

"I'll do my best."

Now that the Inn was finally in view, she slowed her pace and began to stroll to the restaurant, trying to catch her breath.

As she got closer, she forced herself to look at the building with a critical eye. There were places where it needed some touching up. A fresh coat of paint. One of the windowsills needed to be replaced.

The landscaping around the front door was a little shaggy, a little overgrown. It needed a bit of sprucing up, a little bit of tender loving care.

Kind of like herself, she supposed. Now that she was twenty-five, she was tired of biding her time, waiting in vain for something new to happen.

Perhaps it really was time to think about doing something different. Going somewhere new. For too long now she'd been everyone's helper and assistant. She'd watched her best friends be courted, fall in love, and get married. Most were expecting their first babies. Some, like Josh and Gretta, already had two children.

Yes, it seemed like everyone had moved forward in their lives except for her.

The sad thing was that there was no need to stay in Sugarcreek any longer. She had plenty of money saved and even her parents' blessing to go find her happiness.

So why hadn't she done anything yet? Was she afraid . . . or still holding out hope that a certain man would finally notice her and see that she was the perfect girl for him?

That she'd actually been the perfect one for years now?

Pushing aside that disturbing thought, she

slipped inside the Sugarcreek Inn and prepared to offer her excuses to Jana Kent, the proprietor.

Her boss was standing by a pair of book-shelves, unboxing more of the knickknacks she'd recently started selling in an attempt to drum up a bit more business and profit for the inn.

Jana paused when she walked by. "Cutting it close today, Miriam."

Glancing up at the clock over the door, Miriam winced. It was ten after nine. Jana had long since given up on Miriam getting to work early or even on time. Now she merely hoped Miriam wouldn't be too late. "I know. Sorry."

"What's today's excuse?" Humor lit Jana's eyes, telling Miriam that while she might feel exasperated, she wasn't mad.

Usually, Miriam came up with an amusing story or fib. Over the years, earthquakes had erupted, washing machines had overflowed, ravenous dogs had invaded her yard.

Today, however, her mind drew a complete blank. "Time simply got away from me this morning."

Jana looked almost disappointed. "That's it?"

Miriam shrugged weakly. "I'll come up with a better excuse tomorrow, I'm sure of it."

"Miriam Zehr. You are one of my best employees and one of my hardest workers. You always offer to help other people, and you never mind staying late. Why is it so hard for you to get here on time?"

There were all kinds of reasons. Miriam wasn't a morning person. She seemed to always sleep in. She hated to get to work early so she waited until the last second to leave her house.

Unfortunately, though, she feared it was her somewhat irrational way of rebelling against the continual routine of her life. Sometimes her frenetic morning journey to work was the biggest excitement of her day.

Inching away, she mumbled, "I'll go put on my apron and get to work."

"Thank you, Miriam."

Hurrying toward the back, Miriam scanned the tables. Quite a few were empty.

And then she noticed He was there. Junior Beiler. All six-foot-two inches of brawn. Blond hair and perfection.

Junior, the object of too many of her daydreams. The boy she'd had a crush on for as long as she could remember. The man she yearned would truly notice her.

Miriam kept walking, trying not to look his way. Trying not to stare. But she did. And as she did, she noticed that he was staring right back at her. More important, she was sure that something like interest glinted in his blue eyes.

Feeling her cheeks flush, she darted into the kitchen. But the moment the doors closed behind her, she let herself smile.

Maybe today, at long last, would be different.

• • •

The moment Junior Beiler saw the kitchen doors swing shut, he grinned at Joe. "You were right, Miriam Zehr works here. I just saw her walk by."

Joe's expression turned smug. "I told you she did."

"She just went into the kitchens." Drumming his fingers on the table, he murmured, "I hope she comes out again soon."

Joe chuckled. "And when she does? Are you actually going to talk to her about what's been on your mind?"

"Absolutely." Noticing that his buddy's expression looked skeptical, he straightened his shoulders a bit. "What's wrong with that?"

"Just about everything. You can't simply go asking women about their best friends and expect to get information. It ain't done, ya know."

"Why not?" It made perfect sense to him.

"A woman isn't going to give you information if she doesn't know you."

Junior scoffed. As usual, Joe was making a big deal over nothing. "I've known Miriam for years. We both have, Joe."

"*Jah*, we went to *shool* with her, that's true. And we're all in the same church district. But let me ask you this, when was the last time you actually talked to her?"

"I'm pretty sure I said hello to her at church last Sunday."

14

Joe tilted his head slightly. "Did you? Or did you walk right by like you usually do?"

For the first time, Junior felt vaguely uncomfortable. He was one of eight kids, and he was sandwiched between two girls in his family. Because of that, he'd learned a thing or two about the female mind over the years. "I might have only thought about saying hello," he said grudgingly.

Joe looked triumphant. "See?"

Okay, Joe probably had a point. But his inattentiveness didn't mean he didn't like Miriam. He just had never thought about her much.

Until he realized she'd recently become good friends with Mary Kate Hershberger. Beautiful Mary Kate Hershberger, who had moved to Sugarcreek in August and had quickly caught his unwavering attention.

Joe grabbed another hot biscuit from the basket on the table and began slathering it with peanut butter spread. "I still think you should get your sister Kaylene to introduce you. After all, Mary Kate is Kaylene's teacher."

"*Nee.* Kaylene is having trouble in school." Lowering his voice, he said, "Actually, I'm not certain Kaylene is all that fond of her new teacher."

"Don't see why that matters."

"It does." His youngest sister was eight years

old and the apple of his eye. There was no way he was going to use little Kaylene in order to get a date.

"Why?"

Luckily, the kitchen doors swung open again, and out came Miriam. She now had on a white apron over her dress, and was holding a coffeepot in her right hand. Seizing his chance, he turned his coffee cup right side up, waited until she was looking his way, and motioned her over.

Joe raised his brows. "Impressive," he muttered.

When she got to their table, her cheeks were flushed. "*Kaffi?*"

"*Jah*. For both of us."

After she'd filled both their cups, Joe gave him a little kick.

Thinking quickly, Junior asked, "So, Miriam, how have you been?"

She looked a bit startled by the question. "Me? I've been *gut*. Why do you ask?"

"No reason. It's just that, well . . . I mean, I haven't seen you around lately."

She looked at him curiously. "Where have you been looking?"

"Nowhere. I mean, I guess I haven't seen you anywhere but at *gmay*, at church. And here," he added, feeling like a fool.

Joe groaned as he took another bite of biscuit.

"Why were you looking? Did you need something?" Miriam asked.

His tongue was starting to feel like it was too big for his mouth. "Actually, ah . . . yes!" Seizing the opportunity, he added, "I've been wantin' to talk to you about something."

She set the coffeepot right on the table. "You have?"

"Yes. When do you get off work? Can I stop by?"

"You want to come by my house? Tonight?" Her cheeks pinkened.

"I do. May I come over?"

"You may . . . if you'd like. I'll be off work at four."

"*Gut.* I'll stop over around six."

"Do you need my address?"

"No, I know where you live. I'll see you then."

Miriam picked up the coffeepot, smiled shyly, then walked on.

When they were alone again, Junior picked up his coffee cup and took a fortifying sip. "See, Joe? That wasn't so hard."

"It wasn't so *gut.*"

"Really?"

Joe leaned back in his chair and folded his arms across his chest. "You, Junior, are an idiot."

"What are you talking about? I'm going to go over to Miriam's house tonight and talk to her about Mary Kate. It's a *gut* plan. *Wunderbaar.*"

After making sure Miriam wasn't nearby to overhear, Joe hissed, "Miriam doesna think

17

you're coming over to ask about Mary Kate. She thinks you're going courting. How do you think she's going to feel when she discovers that you only want her help to get Mary Kate's attention?"

For the first time, Junior was starting to realize that he should have thought things through a bit more. "Oh. Well, I didn't think of that. I guess . . . the way I asked . . . It's not going to go well, is it?"

"Nope. You've truly made a mess of it. This is not good, Junior."

Warily, Junior glanced in the direction Joe was looking. Spied Miriam.

Noticed that she was standing near the hostess station. Her light blue eyes were bright with happiness. She was smiling softly.

Meeting her gaze, he felt his neck flush.

He had a sudden feeling that Joe was right. And that was not good.

Definitely not good at all.

Chapter Two

This had to be the best day of her entire life.

After twenty-five years of hoping and praying for a change, of doing her best to be happy for her girlfriends when they'd fallen in love, after trying diets and hair tonics unsuccessfully to try to improve her looks, it had happened.

The boy she'd always wanted had finally looked her way.

God had finally answered her prayers! "*Danke*, Got," she whispered. For a moment, she considered reminding Him that she probably hadn't needed to wait quite so long for His blessings . . . but she decided against that.

After all, anyone who was anyone knew that the Lord worked in mysterious ways.

Standing behind one of the stainless steel counters in the kitchen, Miriam couldn't stop smiling. She wasn't sure what she'd done to finally attract the attention of Junior Beiler, but she wasn't about to question her good fortune. After years of looking at him longingly, he'd finally looked back.

And now he was coming to call that very evening!

Across the vast commercial kitchen, her three coworkers kept glancing at her curiously. Finally,

Marla spoke. "I've never seen you so happy to roll out piecrust. Why are you in such a *wonderful-gut* mood?"

Miriam was tempted to share her news. Marla was a good friend, just a few years older than herself, and recently married. Miriam knew that she'd relish hearing about a new romance. But even more tempting was the chance to hold Junior's sudden interest close to her heart.

After all, there would be plenty of time for everyone to comment about their relationship when he took her out walking or for a buggy ride.

"I'm *frayt* today, that's all," she said airily.

Marla exchanged glances with Ruth and Christina. "Do you believe that our Miriam is simply happy, girls?"

"Not even for a minute," Ruth answered, even though, at fifty, she was far from a girl. Ruth had been married, widowed, and now worked at the Sugarcreek Inn beside them in a way that made Miriam forget that she hadn't always been there. And even though Ruth was English and favored faded jeans and T-shirts instead of dresses, aprons, and *kapps*, she was definitely one of their gang. "Come on, Miriam, give us a hint. Jana is in quite the mood today. Every time she comes in here, she fusses. Tell us something good."

Miriam grabbed a handful of flour and took her time spreading it on the counter. "You all make too much of things. I'm merely happy,

that's all. There's nothing wrong with that."

"There is if it's a plain old Thursday in September. Which it is," Ruth declared as she poured three cups of cream into the electric mixer. "I know, you've finally booked one of those trips you're always talking about. Which one are you going on? The weekend in Shipshewana? The bus tour to Colorado?"

"My happiness has nothing to do with trips."

Christina Kempf, twenty-two and adorable, looked over her shoulder while she did the dishes at the sink. As usual, her white *kapp* and violet dress looked as neat as a pin. "Does it involve a boy?"

Miriam wanted to continue to play it cool, but Christina's question made her toss the rest of her resolve out the window.

These were some of her best friends. If she couldn't share her news with them, she didn't know who she'd share the news with.

"Yes," she finally announced with a broad smile. "Yes, it does. The best thing just happened when I went out to the dining room to pour coffee. It was so *wonderful-gut* I can hardly believe it."

Ruth turned off the mixer. "Well, don't keep us in suspense. Tell us!"

"And be quick about it, Miriam," Marla said with a broad grin. "I'm already imagining all kinds of things."

Miriam breathed deep. "Junior Beiler asked if he could stop by my house tonight," she blurted in a rush. "He said he has something he wanted to talk to me about."

After turning off the faucet, Christina rushed to her side. "Oh, Miriam, he's going courting!"

"I think so," Miriam agreed. "After all, why else would he want to come over to my *haus*?"

"I certainly can't think of another reason," Ruth said.

Christina squeezed Miriam's hands, her own getting covered in flour as she did so. "Junior is so handsome. He has such blue eyes, too."

Miriam nodded. Though her eyes were also blue, they certainly weren't the bright blue shade his were. "I know."

"And his hair is so blond."

"I know." She'd always thought his blond hair was attractive. Much better than her mousy brown.

"I'm not sure who he is," Ruth admitted. "Maybe I should go out to the dining room and get a good look at him."

"*Nee!*" Miriam protested. "If you go out there you'll stare at him. I know it."

"I'm not that bad."

"Yes, you are," Marla said.

Still so happy to share her news, Miriam almost squealed. "I could scarcely believe it when he motioned me over to his table. I thought he only wanted *kaffi* . . . but he wanted to chat with me!"

"I'm so happy for you," Marla said. "You've got such a good heart. I'm glad Junior has finally taken notice of you."

"Me, too," Miriam whispered to herself. Now that her big news had been shared, the four of them went back to work, Miriam still feeling like she was on cloud nine.

Then the kitchen doors opened and Jana glared at them all. "I could hear your laughter from the dining room! Just because Valerie is here to wait tables, it doesn't mean you all can do nothing in here."

Before any of them had a chance to point out that they'd been working, Jana snapped, "Whose turn is it to clear tables?"

Miriam raised her hand. "Mine, I'm afraid. I'm sorry. I'll go right out and do that."

"Honestly, Miriam, I don't pay you to come in late and stand around the kitchen chatting. I suggest you get yourself together before you lose this job."

Stung, Miriam rushed out to the dining room and hastily started clearing the tables.

Normally, the harsh words from her boss would have rattled her more. But today, nothing could spoil her good mood.

She hoped the day would fly by, since she was certain that the evening was going to be special.

At last, her life was going to change. She was sure of it.

Chapter Three 🍂

The doctor glanced at Judith in obvious sympathy. "I truly am sorry to have to give you this news, Judith. Though the tests we ran do indicate that your body has recovered from the miscarriage, I cannot in good conscience recommend that you attempt another pregnancy. It would be too dangerous for you. And, I'm sorry to say, your chances of carrying a baby full term are slim."

Judith Knox's heart felt like it had broken into a million pieces. Reaching out, she gripped her husband's hand as hard as she could.

Perhaps if she never let Ben go, she could make it through the next few minutes without completely falling apart.

Ben tensed. "But Judith is all right? I mean, she is going to be all right?"

Dr. Wallace nodded. "Yes, Mr. Knox. Your wife will be just fine, once she recovers completely."

Around a ragged sigh, Ben whispered, "*Danke, Got.*"

Judith knew her husband was grateful, and that his prayer was a good one. She was glad that her body was healing like it should.

But that didn't change the truth, the only truth that Judith could hear right now. Forcing herself to meet the kind English doctor's gaze, Judith murmured, "So, it's over."

"There are other ways to have a family, Judith," the doctor said kindly. "When you're ready, we can talk about that."

"That's not what I want." Looking down at her light gray dress and apron, she squeezed her eyes shut and prayed for strength. She felt so shaky and uneasy she wasn't sure she was even going to be able to continue the conversation without dissolving into tears. Once she regained her balance, she murmured, "Dr. Wallace, please forgive me. I don't mean to make things harder for you."

"There's no need for you to apologize. I understand. This is a difficult time."

Ben gently wrapped his free arm around her, holding her in the most comforting of embraces. "*Doktah*, are you sure about this? I'm no doctor, but it seems to me that many women are still able to have babies after a miscarriage."

"That is true, Ben, but Judith has an unusual situation." In the blink of an eye, Dr. Wallace once again started spouting scientific data and percentages. Enzymes and something about scar tissue, too.

It was much of the same information the doctor had just said a few minutes before, but even the second time, it was just as confusing and difficult to hear.

Judith let the words flow over her, barely listening to the doctor's answers to Ben's carefully thought-out questions.

All she really cared about was the doctor's conclusion—that she would never have a baby of her own. As the eldest girl of seven children, she'd been anticipating motherhood all her life. Now she was going to have to let that dream fade away.

And worse, she was unable to give Ben the perfect family he'd always longed for. A chance for him to be the father his father never was.

Her body had failed them both.

At long last, Dr. Wallace walked to the examining room door. "I am very sorry, Judith. I cannot tell you how much I wish I had different news to tell you." Pausing with her hand on the door handle, she added, "I believe God has a reason for everything. Perhaps one day we'll know why He made this decision."

When they were alone in the room, Ben quietly got to his feet, crossed the room and plucked a pair of tissues from the box next to the sink. After handing them to her, he held out his hand. "Let's go home, Judith. You'll feel better once we're back in Sugarcreek."

She wiped her eyes and followed him out the door. She kept her composure as best she could, while he paid the receptionist, then guided her down the quiet hall.

When their English driver arrived, she allowed Ben to help her into the back of the van. She looked out the window while he told the driver that they'd changed their minds about going out to lunch. That it would be best to simply return to Sugarcreek.

When they got to their home, the two-story house that Ben had grown up in but was now theirs, Judith attempted to smile politely while the driver chatted about the weather and the opening of the new ice cream parlor next to the library.

Once inside, she did her best to pretend that she wasn't devastated. She knelt down and patted their two cats and let the dog outside. She opened the refrigerator, pretending that she actually cared what she was going to make for lunch.

But before she could pull out the fixings for chicken and dumplings, Ben pulled her into his arms. "Leave it," he said. "Come here and let me hold you."

"Oh, Ben." Then, at last, the dam burst. Her tears flowed, and she let herself cry.

After a bit, he guided her to their couch, the one they'd inherited from her parents, which had more than a few lumps. Pulling her close, she rested her cheek on his chest.

And then, to her shame, she cried some more.

"It's going to be all right, Judith," he murmured

as she cried and cried. "We'll get through this, I promise we will."

"It's not going to ever be all right." Pushing herself backward, she scooted a little away, far enough away so that she could see his face while she whispered what was in her heart. "Oh, Ben. I am so sorry. I've failed you."

Those hazel eyes she'd always loved blinked in confusion. Then he shook his head as he gently wiped her damp cheeks with yet another tissue. "Never that. You make me happy, Judith. Always."

"But I know you wanted a baby."

"Stop apologizing. All I care about is you. *Jah*, I did want a *boppli*. But when you miscarried? All I worried about was you. After loving you most of my life, finally you are my wife. I don't want anything to happen to you."

"I am going to be fine."

"And I am mighty glad for that. Judith, your happiness is all I care about right now. If I had lost you? Why, I would have been lost myself. . . ."

Two weeks ago, when she'd started bleeding it had been terrible. And losing their baby had been the worst of situations. But through it all, she'd held tight the knowledge that one day they would hold a baby of their own. She knew several women who had suffered miscarriages but had eventually had perfectly healthy babies.

But now that dream was gone.

"I don't know what I'm going to do now," she whispered.

"We don't need to decide anything right now. All we need to do is rest for a bit."

Decide? There wasn't anything to decide. The decision had been made. What Ben didn't understand was how this changed *everything*.

With a shaky voice, she finally admitted the awful truth. "Ben, all my life I've wanted children. I've wanted to be a mother."

"I know."

Lowering her voice she finally found the courage to whisper, "I truly have no idea what is going to become of me if I'm not a mother."

"You'll be my *frau*. My partner. All I've ever wanted was for you to be mine."

His words were wonderful, and she knew he meant every word. And, of course, she loved him, too. But that didn't stop the ache she felt. "What if that's not enough for me? What am I going to do then?"

He stared at her in shock, tears filling his eyes as he slowly comprehended just how lost she was. "We'll just have to make sure it is," he stated.

"But—"

His voice hardened. "Judith Knox, you listen to me. You need to put these doubts away. For now, I'll do the thinking for both of us." When she tried to draw farther away, he pulled her closer and wrapped his arms around her back.

"I will do the thinking," he repeated, his voice hoarse with emotion. "I will do the thinking and the worrying and the planning. All you have to do is rest and lean on me."

"For how long?"

"For as long as it takes for you to feel better," he said fiercely. "That's how long."

Because he needed her to, she leaned against him and closed her eyes. She rested her head against his firm, solid chest and attempted to breathe slowly and evenly.

After a minute, as if he realized that she wasn't going to leave their embrace, his hands gentled. He sighed and pressed his lips to the top of her head. Little by little, she felt his muscles relax.

Because she knew him so well, she knew he was hoping things were better now. That she was going to follow his advice and lean on him. That one day soon she'd be back to her regular self.

She dreaded the moment when he realized that wasn't going to happen.

Chapter Four ✦

Albert Beiler had been called Junior all of his life. He'd been called Junior for so long, he'd even stopped wondering where the nickname came from. He wasn't named after his father, so he wasn't a "junior" anything.

At least, not that he could figure out.

He was the eldest boy in a family of eight children. He was child number two, stuck in between Claire and Beverly. After Beverly, there was a two-year gap, then came Micah, Randall, Neil, and Levi. Eight years younger than Levi was little Kaylene.

Kaylene was his parents' surprise, and her eldest brother's heart. Actually, she was most everyone's favorite, and it was no secret why.

After Kaylene's birth, their mother had never really recovered. She'd refused to go to the doctor, refused to accept her weakness post-delivery. Then, one sunny day in July, she'd collapsed.

She'd passed away soon after at the hospital.

Then, when Kaylene was just four years old, their father had died from a heart attack, forcing Junior to become the man of the house.

That was four years ago.

Now, he and Claire and Beverly had become

something of a triumvirate. Together, the three of them did their best to guide their brothers and raise their sister.

Luckily, all of the boys were now out of school and doing various jobs . . . enabling Junior to not feel the complete burden of providing for the family.

He'd always thought the Lord had provided little Kaylene with her own set of guardian angels. There was really no other reason that he could think for her to be so well-adjusted.

Though a little shy, she was a sweet child, and seemed to lean on each of them in different ways.

But it was generally agreed that she depended on him the most.

He'd never minded that.

If he was around, Junior made sure Kaylene never had to wait too long to be noticed. He'd taken it upon himself to look out for her. To make sure she got her hugs and ate her supper. He made sure she'd gotten a kitten to cuddle at night since she had a room all to herself.

And that she always knew he was on her side. No matter what.

Which was maybe why it was she who rushed out to see him the moment he'd finished putting Princess—the somewhat homely horse with the fancy name Kaylene had given her—in her stable. If Kaylene knew anything, it was that her eldest brother always had time to spare for her.

"Hiya, Kay," he said as he picked up the curry-comb. Pushing aside his thread of worry about his upcoming visit to Miriam, he smiled at his littlest sister. "How are you today?"

"*Gut.*" Walking closer, she raised her hand to give Princess a gentle rub on her muzzle. "Where have you been?"

"I had some things to take care of in town."

"I didn't know you were going into Sugarcreek."

"That's because you have more important things to think about."

"Like what?"

"Like school." Taking a deep breath, he braced himself to ask her least favorite question. "So, how was *shool* today?"

As was her habit, she started twirling one of the ties from her *kapp* around a finger. "I don't know."

He glanced her way as he carefully worked on Princess's coat. The mare enjoyed the attention, tossing her head a bit as he gently combed her mane.

And still Junior waited. His sister had something on her mind, and she was obviously biding her time until she said her piece.

Giving her a prod, he asked, "What have you been doing since you got home this afternoon?"

"My chores."

"Did you get them done?"

"Uh-huh." After releasing the tie, she kicked at the dirt under her foot.

He moved around to Princess's other side and started brushing her coat in earnest. "I know sweeping the front porch didn't take too long. What else have you been doing?"

She wrinkled her nose. "My homework."

"And what is your homework?"

"Reading."

The word was uttered with such disdain that Junior was tempted to grin. At last, he'd discovered what had made her so upset. "And how is that going?"

After a moment's pause, she looked at her feet. "You know, Junior."

She was right, he did know.

"Come on. Let's go sit down." After giving the mare one last friendly pat, he guided Kaylene to a bench next to the back door of the barn. He liked sitting out there because it was out of the line of vision of the house. One could sit there for a few minutes without being detected— which was no small thing in a house of eight.

With a sigh, his little sister scrambled up beside him and tried to look very brave.

Which melted his heart, of course. "Reading ain't getting any easier for you?"

After a pause, she shook her head. "We have to count the pages we've read and write them in a notebook. And then we have to write a sentence about what we read."

"That doesn't sound too hard."

Lowering her voice, she said, "Junior, I have the smallest amount of pages in the whole class. Everyone knows it, too."

Kicking his feet out, he tried to think of the best way to approach her problem. On one hand, he was proud of her honesty. Any one of her older brothers would have simply fibbed about the number of pages read.

And if she had done that, it would have certainly spared her the embarrassment. But of course that wasn't the problem. Her problem was that she'd always struggled with reading.

"Have you talked to Beverly or Claire about this?"

"Uh-huh."

Hope filled him. "And? What did they say?"

Kaylene averted her eyes. "That I need to try harder."

"Ah." He was a bit surprised, though he shouldn't be. Claire and Beverly had always excelled in school and had never been known for their patience. They were wonderful women, and looked out for the rest of their siblings like formidable mother hens.

But neither was the type to coddle Kaylene or her older brothers about school. Beverly and Claire, like him, had a fairly vivid memory of their parents. Though they'd been very kind and had enjoyed spending time with their children, neither had been especially cuddly people. They'd had high standards for the Beiler children and little patience for excuses.

And that had probably been a good thing, especially for his four younger brothers, who were a handful even on the best of days. But with sweet Kaylene? He tended to think that was the wrong approach.

She was different from the rest of them. She was a lot more hesitant. Needed a lot more hugs and gentle words.

And with school, she needed lots of reassurance; otherwise her doubts and worries got the best of her.

Though most of his friends growing up would have been surprised, Junior was the one in the household who had a seemingly endless supply of patience with the littlest member of their family.

"Kay, what do you think we should do?"

"I got to learn to read better, Junior."

"Your teacher can't help?"

After another pause, she shook her head. "Miss Mary Kate says I'm just slow."

"She said that?"

"Uh-huh. She said even though I do things a little later than most, she thinks one day I'm gonna be just as smart as the rest of you. That is, if I try real hard."

Inwardly, Junior winced. He was surprised Mary Kate would say something like that. Though he was just getting to know her, he would have thought a teacher would be a bit more understanding about one of her students' reading problems. Or at least a little more tactful. "What do you think about what she said?"

Clasping her hands tightly on her lap, Kaylene shook her head. "I don't think I'll ever be as smart as Beverly. And I know I'll never be as smart as Micah."

He chuckled. "I don't think any of us will be." Micah was the brightest of them all. He'd been reading big books by the time he was eight or nine, and there hadn't been a math or science problem he couldn't figure out.

Years ago, when they'd all been much closer to Kaylene's current age, their parents had announced that Micah had made them mighty proud. That he could be absolutely anything he wanted to be. He could start his own Amish business or even possibly be a doctor if he didn't join their faith.

"Would you like me to visit with Mary Kate? See if she has any suggestions?"

After a moment's pause, she gave a little nod. "You don't mind?"

"I don't mind." Though some outside the family would say it wasn't a brother's job to worry about a sister's reading ability, none of his siblings would be surprised. Kaylene didn't have parents of her own, and she needed her siblings to fill that role. He would do just about anything to help his little sister. And, well, Miss Mary Kate just happened to be Miss Mary Katherine Hershberger, the woman he was going to ask Miriam about.

Warming up to the idea, he thought this might give him even more opportunities to get to know Mary Kate. Who knew? Maybe getting to know Mary Kate better would encourage her to be more patient with his little sister.

At last, Kaylene's expression brightened. "*Danke*, Junior," she said with a smile. "You really are the nicest one in the whole family."

Unfortunately, her statement had the opposite effect than what she'd no doubt intended. It made him remember just how awkward it was going to be when he saw Miriam later tonight. If Joe was right, she had no idea he was going to visit merely to get help with another girl. When she realized that, her feelings were certainly going to be hurt.

Giving his sister a little pat on her back, he said, "I'll stop by the school tomorrow afternoon. Try not to worry, Kay. We'll get things figured out."

After a brief hug, his little sister went back to the house. He took the opportunity to spend a few minutes by himself. To figure out how he was going to set things right with Miriam.

Chapter Five ⨍

"Where are you and Junior planning to sit when he comes over? It's a little too chilly to visit outside, don'tcha think?" her mother asked as she entered Miriam's bedroom.

"I guess I'll bring him into the living room." Miriam shrugged, pretending his visit didn't matter to her all that much. Though she'd been staring at the same page of her novel for the last fifteen minutes, she certainly didn't need her mother discovering that. Her *mamm* would become even more excited about her caller. Miriam had purposefully gone into her bedroom to read in an effort to appear nonchalant.

"*Jah*, I suppose that will be the best spot for him," her mother agreed, looking distracted and a bit anxious. "Just so you know, I put some of the cookies you made this morning on a plate."

"*Danke*. We have *tay* and lemonade, too. I'll ask Junior if he wants anything to drink."

"I'll get out the glasses. Should I make *kaffi*?"

Getting up from her rocking chair, Miriam shook her head. "*Nee*, Mamm. And please, don't do anything more. I'll take care of the glasses and such. Junior's only coming over for a bit. It's nothing to get too excited about."

The look her mother gave her said she disagreed with that statement. Completely.

"Miriam, I know it's been a while, but a man expects to be welcomed into a house when he goes courting."

She would have laughed if her mother's words weren't so expected or so serious. "Everything will go fine, Mamm. Besides, he didn't act like he was planning to stay long. Only that he wanted to talk to me about something."

"And we both know what that 'something' must be, don't we?"

Miriam said nothing, but she had a feeling her mother was right. She could only imagine one reason for Junior Beiler to talk to her in private, and at her house, no less! Feeling some of the same restlessness that her mother did, she carefully took off her *kapp* and took down her hair.

Her mother crossed her arms over her chest and watched her, a winsome expression playing across her face.

Now she was starting to feel a bit foolish. "I'll be out soon."

Her mother's lips curved as she watched Miriam brush her hair, then repin it neatly under her white *kapp*. "I have to say that I'm mighty happy for you, dear. For years I've been waiting for you to have callers. I was starting to wonder when that day would come."

Years! Nothing like a mother's honesty to put

things into perspective! "Me, too, Mamm."

After another meaningful look her way, her mother pattered back down the hall, finally leaving Miriam alone with her thoughts. Her jumbled, silly, exasperated thoughts.

She did love her parents so much. But she was a late-in-life child, born almost ten years after her brother and sister. She'd barely started school when they'd been in the midst of their *rumspringa*. She'd been struggling with her cursive when they'd both become baptized and engaged.

Now each had families of their own. Her sister, Teresa, had four children, and her brother, Nolan, had two.

Over the years, her parents had been spending more and more time with Teresa and Nolan and their families. Now that they were retired, it wasn't unusual for them to spend a week with Nolan in Medina and then another week with Teresa and her family in Middlefield.

Miriam had never blamed their choices. She knew in many ways she was a riddle to her parents. They'd never intended to raise a constantly late, somewhat dreamy girl who would rather stick her nose in a book or bake pies than be at a singing or gathering of young people.

Of course, much of the reason she'd read so much was because most of the boys had never spared her a second glance. No matter how hard she'd tried, her hair had never lain smoothly under her *kapp*. No matter how many times she said no to dessert she never lost weight.

She'd been a wallflower, waiting on the sidelines for something, anything, to happen. After a while, she stopped going to avoid the disappointment.

But now it looked like things were about to change. Her father seemed relieved, her mother was pleased as punch, and Miriam was struggling with the unusual feeling of doing something that her mother was pleased about.

Or perhaps, it was more the feeling of relief that came from actually "being" the daughter her mother wanted.

Shaking off that bit of melancholy, she glanced at the time, saw that Junior was sure to arrive in a few minutes, and scurried to the living room. Once there, she lit two of the kerosene lamps, carefully set the plate of cookies on the coffee table, then filled two glasses with ice.

Just as Junior knocked at the door.

After sharing a somewhat anxious look with her mother, her *mamm* walked back to the kitchen and Miriam let Junior inside.

"*Wilcom*," she said as she stared up at him in the doorway. He looked much the same as he had at the restaurant, though he'd changed shirts. This one was white.

"*Danke*." He took off his hat, then stepped

inside, seeming to swallow the oxygen as he filled the room. Junior looked at her, at the plate of cookies on the coffee table, then practically crushed the rim of his hat in his hands. "Thank you for letting me come over."

Letting him? That seemed like an odd choice of words. For the first time, a bit of unease filtered through her. She'd imagined he'd be all smiles, maybe even teasing her a bit, like she'd seen him do with his family and friends.

Instead, he wasn't even smiling. Only standing awkwardly. She took things into her own hands. "Junior, please have a seat. Would you like a glass of lemonade or tea?"

He looked as if he were about to refuse, but nodded instead. "*Tay*, if you don't mind."

If she didn't mind? She'd offered!

"I don't mind at all. Um, I'll be right back." Needing to take a moment to gather her thoughts, she took her time walking the few steps to the kitchen. Steadfastly ignoring her parents' questioning looks, she poured tea into the two prepared glasses, took a deep breath, then entered the sitting room again.

Junior was eating a cookie. "These are *gut*, Miriam."

"*Danke.*"

"Are they oatmeal raisin?"

She would have thought that was obvious. "*Jah.*"

43

"You ah, bake a lot, hmm? Someone at the restaurant told me that you bake a lot of the pies and rolls."

"I enjoy baking." She set both glasses on the table, then opted to sit on one of the sturdy chairs across from him. She needed the distance from him, and she also felt like she needed to be able to look at him directly. There was something not quite right about this visit, but she couldn't put her finger on why she felt that way.

Junior bit into the cookie again, chewed.

She took a sip of tea. Crossed her legs. Waited almost patiently.

Finally, he leaned forward, his elbows resting on his knees. "Miriam, we've known each other a long time."

"Years," she agreed, smiling encouragingly.

"*Jah.*" He sat back, looking more uncomfortable with each passing second. "Um. I know we've never been the best of friends, but I've always thought that we could be, you know?"

No, she didn't. Actually, his words were a complete surprise to her.

Though she'd always had something of a crush on him, it had been perfectly obvious that he'd never spared a second thought for her.

For the last few years, she'd racked her brain, trying to figure out how she could be the type of person he wanted to know well.

She ached to tell him that. To ask him why he

hadn't ever wanted to know her better. To ask him what she'd done that had finally changed his mind.

But all of that seemed like it would make things even more awkward.

"Junior, you seem a little nervous."

"I'm not *naerfich*, it's just that I have something I wanted to talk to you about, but I'm afraid it's going to come as a surprise."

"It might not be as much of a surprise as you might imagine," she said as encouragingly as possible. "Why don't you just ask me what you wanted to? After all, you are exactly right. We have known each other a long time."

"All right. Well, like I said, I came over here to talk to you about something."

"Yes?" She leaned forward a bit. Encouragingly.

He met her eyes, frowned, then seemed to fixate upon a spot just above her head. "I wanted to talk to you about Mary Katherine Hershberger."

All day she'd been thinking about his visit. All day she'd been imagining what he would say, how he would look.

How he would look at her.

She had never imagined he would want to discuss another woman. "What about Mary Kate?"

"I heard you were good friends with her." His gaze drifted down. Found hers. Fastened on tight. "Is that true?"

A sudden, horrible foreboding coursed through her as she began to realize why he'd come over. "*Jah*, that is true. I mean, as good friends as two people can be who just met a few months ago." Feeling dread and a slow suspicion burning in her stomach, she stared. "Why?"

For the first time he smiled. His smile lit up his face, highlighted his two perfect dimples. "Well, I'm interested in her, you see." His voice brightened. "And the two times I've tried to talk to her haven't gone so well. She seemed a little disinterested."

"Disinterested?"

"*Jah*. Is she seeing someone that I'm not aware of?"

Little by little, the true purpose of his visit sank in. He'd been thinking about Mary Kate, not her. He wanted to court Mary Kate. Not her. In the blink of an eye, she was a wallflower again.

With effort, she pushed her disappointment away and answered him. "I don't think Mary Kate is seeing anyone, Junior."

His brows rose. "Are you sure about that? I thought all women talked about things like that."

"Unfortunately, we have not." She cleared her throat. "I don't think Mary Kate is seeing someone, though she may have a man in her life I don't know anything about."

"I doubt that," he said, looking more than a little relieved. "Miriam, I'm hoping you can help me a bit. Maybe if Mary Kate sees that we're friends, she'll want to get to know me better."

"Are we friends, Junior?"

"I would like to be."

He wanted to be her *"freind."* In order to get another woman to notice him.

This couldn't be happening. Her parents were in the other room, practically planning her wedding. Her mother was going to be crushed when she discovered the true reason for Junior's visit.

But far more important than her mother's reaction was the sharp sting of embarrassment that was flooding through her. She'd been sure that with age would come something else, something close to confidence, or at least that she'd be smarter.

Instead, she'd allowed herself to become hopeful that her sweetest dream would come true.

Junior's neck turned red as the seconds passed. "Have I upset you? Joe told me asking you was a mighty bad idea."

"He did?" Joe had just risen in her estimation.

"Jah. I'm, ah, sorry if you thought I came over here for another reason. If I gave you the wrong impression."

Oh, he had.

But she'd taken that idea and run with it, practically telling the whole world that Junior had finally come courting. Why couldn't she have kept her big mouth shut?

"Joe said I shouldn't bother you about Mary Kate, but I didn't know who else to ask. Since she only moved to Sugarcreek recently, not too many people know her well. Except you."

Oh, but this was horrible. Now they both knew that she was disappointed. She needed to say something and soon!

"I . . . ah, am surprised about your interest in Mary Kate," she allowed. Then paused. Was so, so tempted to tell him to go get his own girl-friends.

But where Junior Beiler was concerned, it seemed she couldn't do anything but abuse herself. "But, of course, I'll be happy to help you get to know her if I can."

The tense lines on his forehead relaxed. "You will? That's great." Leaning forward, he asked, "What do you think we should do?"

Carefully pushing aside her misery, she said, "Maybe the three of us could sit together at lunch after church one day?"

"She wouldn't find that strange?"

It wasn't any stranger than him coming over to ask for her help with Mary Kate! "*Nee* . . . not if she thought we were friends."

"You're right. And we are friends. Maybe even better friends now." Looking like he'd just won a million dollars, he hopped to his feet. "*Danke,*

Miriam," he said as he gave her a little awkward pat on the shoulder. "I knew coming over here to talk to you about this was the right decision."

"I'm glad you came over," she lied. Actually, at the moment, she couldn't wait for him to leave. She needed space. Watching his hand hover over the plate of cookies, she handed him a napkin. "Please, take a couple of cookies home with you."

"You wouldn't mind?"

"Not at all." She'd give him the plate if she could. Anything to move him on. "I, ah, bake a lot of cookies."

He grabbed three, folded them in the napkin, then strode to the door. "See you *Sunndawk*," he said with a smile. "I'll find you after the service."

She forced herself to return the happy look. "Yes! Sunday!"

She kept the smile on her face as she closed the door behind him, while she dimmed the lights in the front room, and as she carried the two glasses back to the kitchen.

Her mother was hovering by the kitchen counter when she entered. "I heard, Miriam," she said excitedly, practically pouncing on her. "He wants to see you on Sunday! I'm so thrilled for you. Junior is such a nice boy. Not every young man could take charge of a family the way he has."

There were two choices she could make. Either admit that Junior had no use for her, other than as a way to get her best friend's attention.

Or she could keep the bad news to herself.

Only one of those options was going to give her any peace. "*Jah*. We are going to sit together for a bit after church."

"I'm so happy for you, daughter," her father said. "I told your mother that it was only a matter of time before you had a caller. You were just a late bloomer, that's all."

A headache was coming on. Due, no doubt, to the enormous effort it was taking to lie and conceal her true thoughts. "You were right, Daed. It was just a matter of time."

"Tomorrow, I'm going to call Teresa and let her know your news. Your sister's been so worried about your lack of callers." With a wry chuckle, her mother added, "Believe it or not, Teresa was actually starting to think something was wrong with you."

"There's nothing wrong with me."

"Of course not. That little bit of extra weight you've been carrying hasn't done you a bit of harm. Now that handsome Junior Beiler has set his sights on you, nothing is wrong at all!" Her mother pressed a slim, cool hand on her bare arm. "This is your time now, dear. Your time."

Miriam tried to smile. When she walked back into the front room, she saw the plate of cookies.

Thought about her mother's sly comment about her extra weight.

Thought of Mary Kate's naturally slim figure and quiet beauty.

As she grabbed three cookies and walked upstairs, Miriam realized she'd rarely felt so helpless or empty.

All her life, she'd done her best to do what was right. She worked. She was a dutiful daughter. She'd helped her friends prepare for their weddings. She'd tried to be a good friend to just about everyone.

But instead of it bringing her many blessings, at the moment, she felt like she was merely being overlooked yet again.

What if it was never going to be "her time"? What would she do then?

She popped one of the cookies in her mouth and chewed slowly. And tried not to care.

Chapter Six ✻

Friday morning arrived with a cool wind and the unexpected warmth of the sun. The previous fall had been especially cold. They'd gotten snow in September and it had stayed cold most of the fall.

This year's fall was a welcome change. So far they'd had more warm days than cool ones. Junior and his brothers had been taking advantage of the warm weather, spending the majority of their days outside, mending fencing, plowing fields, cutting back brush.

This morning, Junior had been focused on repairing some fencing around his mother's garden.

The small job had been perfect for his head and heart. He needed some time to think.

Over and over, he'd replayed his visit to Miriam's. Sometimes he felt guilty, because he'd known he'd disappointed her, even though Miriam had tried to pretend otherwise.

Other times, he would half convince himself that he'd done nothing wrong. It wasn't his fault that he didn't fancy Miriam. The Lord worked in mysterious ways, and for whatever reason, He hadn't seen fit to make them the right people for each other.

There was nothing Junior could do about that.

And though he felt a bit guilty about bringing the Lord into his love life, Junior was discovering that he was willing to do whatever it took to ease his troubled, mixed-up head.

When he wasn't telling himself that the Lord was on his side, his thoughts turned a little darker. He turned a little bit more selfish, and a little bit more full of himself. He started telling himself that his rejection of Miriam shouldn't have come as a big surprise.

So therefore, he had nothing to feel guilty about. At all. She shouldn't blame him for a thing. After all, it stood to reason that a spark would have formed between them long ago if there had been anything romantic between them.

But of course, that didn't sit well, either.

He was still thinking about his visit and juggling his feelings about it when Joe stopped by the farm around three.

Joe had yet to admit it, but Junior knew his best friend had a bit of a crush on his sister Beverly. Beverly had shown some interest in Joe, too. But so far, neither had made it much further than chatting about the weather.

Junior imagined that they both were worried about how he would handle a romance between them. They'd be surprised to discover that he thought a romance between them would be a good thing.

Ever since their parents had passed away, Junior felt it was his responsibility to make sure each of his siblings found a match. If Beverly and Joe started courting and eventually married, Junior would only have six more siblings to go.

"So, how did your visit to Miriam's *haus* go?" Joe said by way of greeting.

Junior shrugged. Joe had known him as long as Miriam had. But he wasn't nearly as shy about sharing his opinions. "It went all right, I think. Miriam is going to arrange for her, Mary Kate, and me to eat lunch together after *gmay* on Sunday."

But instead of congratulating Junior on a plan well-played, Joe looked a little bit perturbed. Pulling off his hat, he brushed his dark hair away from his face. "Really? I was sure Miriam had thought you'd come courting. And I was mighty sure she was going to be disappointed when she discovered the truth."

Remembering the spic-and-span front room, the plate of cookies, and the glasses of iced tea, Junior conceded that Joe had a point. But no way was he going to dig into all that with Joe.

"She knows we're just friends. And that that is all we'll ever be." More than ready to get the focus off him, he said, "Kind of like you and Beverly."

But instead of looking embarrassed, Joe merely

smiled. "You know how I feel about your sister. I've never only wanted to be her friend."

Junior pretended to grimace. "Please—"

"Sorry if I'm making you uncomfortable, but I've never made a secret about my feelings. Not to you or Beverly."

"You've told Beverly your thoughts?"

"Of course." With a smirk, he said, "Not everyone waits and waits forever. Some of us go after what we want."

"If you're in a hurry to have Beverly, please, step things up, Joe," he joked. "Quit fussing around and start courting her in earnest."

"I would . . . except that she's been worried about your reaction."

"If you start courting Beverly in earnest, the last thing in the world I'll be is mad. I'll be grateful, that's what I'll be."

"Grateful?"

"Well, if you marry her one day, that will be one less sibling to have to look out for." He kept his voice light, but he was only half teasing.

"You sure take your job as the eldest boy seriously."

"I do, but it's a matter of logistics, too. There's eight of us kids in the house. Most of us adults. Living like this can be fairly cramped." And chaotic. And loud.

Joe laughed. "Want to go inside your kitchen with me and chat with Beverly? You can help

55

spur things along. You know, tell her how wonderful I am and all that."

"As much fun as that sounds, I'm afraid I don't have time for that today. I have a meeting I need to go to. I'm so sorry you'll be missing your opportunity to witness my sparkling personality," Junior quipped. "You could have gotten some tips. For some reason I don't think you'll be needin' my help anyway."

Looking at the front door of the house, Joe raised his brows. "No, I won't be needing any help . . . only Beverly's consent. Where is your meeting?"

"At the *shool*. I promised Kaylene I'd talk to Mary Kate."

"But I thought you didn't want to get Kaylene involved with your love life. Has she decided she wants you and her teacher together?"

"Not at all. This meeting is about my sister."

For a moment, Joe looked like he was going to ask about that, but the idea seemed to float away the moment he noticed Beverly glance at them through the window. Eyes fixated on her, Joe squared his shoulders. "Wish me luck."

"Good luck." Junior watched him enter their house, grinning at the way Joe took off his hat so fast it slipped from his hands. He made a mental note to be sure to have a talk with Beverly about her and Joe soon. If she wanted his approval, he needed her to know she had it.

Still stewing, Junior set out on the short ten-minute walk to the schoolhouse.

Walking to the old schoolhouse brought back a hundred memories. Unlike Kaylene, when he'd been in school, many of his siblings had gone there at the same time. They'd walked together in a pack of sorts. He and Claire and Beverly and Randall. For his last few years, Micah and even Neil had been there, too. Though they'd all had different strengths and struggles academically, they'd had something in common as well: a gregariousness mixed with a competitive streak.

But they'd also been blessed to have the best teacher ever: Miss Hannah. She'd been an old maid and a bit cranky. But she'd been the type of teacher to keep them all in line . . . and had been known to give hugs and affectionate little pats on the back whenever one of them did something especially good.

After Miss Hannah had retired, the school had had a steady stream of teachers. One lady whom no one liked much, then Miss Clara, whom they'd all loved. She'd even stayed on after the first year she'd been married to Tim Graber.

Now, Mary Kate was the teacher. And though she was lovely . . . he was starting to get the feeling that she was never going to be the teacher that Miss Hannah was. Which was a real shame.

But if things went the way he hoped, then she

might quit teaching anyway, to start their own family.

He arrived at the old schoolhouse just as the *kinner* were getting dismissed. Standing under one of the big maple trees that dotted the school yard, he watched the twenty or so boys and girls scamper out of the front door, some laden with books, others carrying lunch boxes and jackets.

His sister was in the thick of them. But unlike most of the other kids, she wasn't laughing or talking a mile a minute. Instead, she looked dejected.

He started to worry. Had she had a bad day? Were the other kids teasing her? Was there something more going on that she hadn't told him about? He was just debating whether he should have gotten Claire or Beverly, or even Randall, involved with things, when one of the kids next to her tapped her on the shoulder and pointed in his direction.

Looking his way, she brightened considerably. He pushed off from the trunk of the tree as she ran over to meet him.

"You came," she said.

"I told you I would." Reaching for her hand, he linked his fingers with hers and walked back in the empty schoolhouse.

The building was dim inside, only lit by the multitude of windows that lined both sides. Off to one side was a sink and a restroom.

On the other was the teacher's desk, two

cabinets, and a row of shelves. The whole place smelled faintly of paste and crayons and the unmistakable scent of children.

In the center of it all stood Mary Katherine. Tall and slim, she captured his attention like nothing else. Today she wore a dark green dress with a matching apron. The sleeves only reached her elbows. She had her back to them, erasing the blackboards. He could have stood and watched her for quite a while, he was so smitten.

Kaylene, however, didn't look to share his feelings. As they stood in silence, her happiness seemed to vanish, and her manner became stiff and worried.

"It will be okay, Kay," he whispered.

"Sure?"

"Mighty sure." Then more loudly, he cleared his throat and called out, "Mary Kate?"

She whipped around, obviously startled. "Kaylene! Hello again, I thought you had left."

"I did, Teacher, but I brought my *bruder* back."

It might have been his imagination, but Junior thought Mary Kate seemed almost afraid.

Staying where he was, he said, "We just got here. I mean, I just did." Because she still looked vaguely uneasy, he attempted a smile. "I'm Junior Beiler, by the way. I'm Kaylene's eldest brother."

"It's nice to meet you," she said politely before

turning to his sister with a look of concern. "Is something wrong, Kaylene?"

Kaylene's hand tightened on his as she obviously struggled for the right words to say.

He spoke up. "We were hoping for a few minutes of your time."

Little by little, the tension in her shoulders eased. She put the eraser down and walked toward them. "Of course."

After picking up a notebook from her desk, she motioned that they sit, pulling out another chair near Kaylene's desk.

Junior was puzzled by her manner. He'd had the vague hope that sparks would fly between them when they had the chance to actually spend some time together. Now, at least, they had something to actually talk about.

Unfortunately, there certainly weren't any sparks at the moment.

Beside him, Kaylene simply sat, looking a bit shy.

As Mary Kate continued to watch and wait, he decided to go ahead and start the ball rolling. "Well. Um . . . Kaylene has been telling me about how she's been having trouble with her reading."

"She is having some trouble, but I feel certain she'll get the hang of things soon. After all, we've been talking about ways to improve, haven't we, Kaylene? You simply need to practice more."

Turning his way, Mary Kate smiled softly. "Junior, I don't think she has a serious problem. She's just fallen behind a bit. I think all she needs is to read a bit more. And perhaps gain some confidence."

Though his pulse jumped from her smile and the use of his name, his heart ached as his little sister bowed her chin in embarrassment. He rested a hand on her shoulder. "She has been practicing, but I think she needs some extra help, too."

"I see."

But the look in her eyes said she didn't "see" his point at all. Instead of seeing compassion and understanding, Junior felt an undercurrent of frustration emanating from Mary Kate.

"We would appreciate some extra help, wouldn't we, Kay?"

She nodded her head. "*Jah.*"

"I'll see what I can do," Mary Kate said. "However, I don't have a lot of extra time."

"I was thinking perhaps you—or someone else—could work with her a bit after school? We've all tried a bit, but you know how things are when working with brothers and sisters. . . ."

Mary Kate nodded curtly. "That is a good idea. I'll ask around."

He was again put off by her vague response, but tried to give her the benefit of the doubt. "*Danke.* That is all we can ask of you, right?" he said with a little smile, certain that was a line Mary Kate said all the time.

But she didn't look to be in any hurry to spout off any words of wisdom. Instead, she got to her feet and pushed in the chairs with a small sigh. "So, is that all you wanted to discuss?"

"*Jah*."

"I'll see you on *Moondawk* then, Kaylene."

"Yes, Teacher."

As Junior felt the meeting coming to a close, he was anxious to prolong their conversation. He glanced back at Mary Kate, struck yet again by how pretty she was. Slim and petite, with auburn hair and green eyes, he was sure he'd never seen a woman as blessed by beauty.

Unable to help himself, he remembered what he and Miriam had discussed. "Perhaps I'll be seeing you at church on Sunday?"

"Perhaps."

"Why only perhaps? Do you not know your Sunday plans yet?" he joked.

"I imagine I'll be going to church. I just wasn't sure if our paths would cross. I hope they do." She smiled, her lips tight.

Mildly encouraged, he turned to his sister. "Kaylene, go outside for a second, wouldja?"

After Kaylene left, Junior turned to Mary Kate. "I was just talking to Miriam about you."

"You were?" She looked wary.

"*Jah*. Ah, Miriam and I have known each other

for years. We're friends. I understand you two are *gut* friends, too?"

"We are." At last her expression eased into a friendly smile. "She's a really nice woman. The best."

Feeling a bit awkward since, of course, he hadn't exactly been being the best of friends to Miriam, he said, "I told her that with you being fairly new here in Sugarcreek, I'd be happy to introduce you to some more folks."

"That is kind of you, but I'm fairly busy."

"Perhaps you'll have a bit of time after church. A group of us gets together to catch up every Sunday. Maybe you'd like to join us?"

"I'm not sure if I'll have time for that."

"I hope you will. I mean, what can it hurt, right?"

When she looked down at her hands instead of answering, Junior finally got the message. She was eager for their conversation to be over. Gripping the brim of his straw hat, he took a step backward. "Well, I'll be seeing you, then . . ."

"*Jah.* Perhaps another day after school. Or on Sunday."

"*Jah.* And thank you for helping Kaylene."

"Your sister is a sweet girl," she replied, her soft voice filling the room. "You don't have to thank me for helping her. Besides, it's my job, *jah*?"

He nodded, aching to say something else, but he was out of ideas.

At last, he turned and walked out to the front picnic table, where Kaylene was waiting for him. He stopped for a moment and injected a bit of false brightness into his voice. "So, are ya ready to go?"

"Yep."

"Let's go, then. Hand me your book bag and I'll carry it."

"You don't have to do that, Junior."

"Carrying book bags is what big brothers are for, Kay," he said lightly. After she handed him the bag, he swung it on his shoulder, then started walking down the familiar path toward home.

Even when they were off the school grounds, his sister was still silent, only looking at her feet as they walked. Junior felt like he should say something. "Well, we took care of things with your teacher, didn't we?"

She shrugged. After a few more steps, she said, "I sure wish I could read better, Junior."

Her voice was wistful. Melancholy. "I know."

"If I could read, then no one will make fun of me."

His heart went out to her . . . just as another part of him was eager to stand up to all the children who were teasing his little sister and give them a piece of his mind. "I promise, I'm sure Mary Kate will help you. And if she can't help ya, why, we've got a whole family to help you."

"Everyone's real busy."

"They are, but everyone loves you, too. We can make time. Together, we will get you reading in no time."

"Promise?" Hope shone in her eyes. Humbling him.

"Of course. And we both know that I never break my promises to you. Never."

"Never ever," she teased.

"That's right. Never ever."

She looked like she was about to say more, but spied Neil in the front yard with his beagle puppy, going through another lesson. "Look, there's Neil! And Bud!"

She took off in front of him, scampering toward their nineteen-year-old brother who'd been born with a way with animals. At the moment, he was raising beagle pups and goats. The second Neil saw Kaylene, he and Bud bounded over to greet her.

Junior slowed his pace. Bud was barking and wagging his tail and Neil was bent over slightly, obviously listening to every bit of Kaylene's report of her day.

There were so many in his family, but somehow they all did their best to make time for one another. He knew without a doubt that every one of them would spend hours helping Kaylene learn to read if that was what it took. At the moment, though, he didn't have the heart to ask everyone to do one more thing. They each had their hands full with the farm and the house and jobs . . . and well, everything.

Besides, he'd decided long ago that he would bear the responsibility of tending to Kaylene's needs.

Mary Kate had a whole class of students to look after. Though he was disappointed about her efforts so far, Junior knew he should give her another opportunity to do everything he'd hoped she would.

And if she didn't? He supposed he would once again push aside his own interests and concentrate on Kaylene's. One day, he knew, she would be grown up and wouldn't need him to fight her battles anymore. But for now? She deserved the best he had.

Chapter Seven ƒ

Mary Kate waited a full twenty minutes after Kaylene and her brother left, then quickly got her things together and locked up. She had to get out of her classroom or she was going to feel like the walls were closing on her. Being in a one-room schoolhouse for eight hours could do that to a girl.

That said, she surely did not want to go straight home to her apartment. Things were too empty there. And quiet.

But, unfortunately, she had few other places in mind to go. Even though she'd been in Sugarcreek almost two months, she still felt as if she didn't fit in.

She would have thought things would have been better by now.

So far, her only really good friend was Miriam Zehr. And though Miriam was wonderful, Mary Kate would have been lying if she said that she was used to having only one girlfriend.

Back in Millersburg, things had been a lot different. She'd been close to her parents and all of her friends. She always had a busy social calendar. Often, her mother would chide her for never making time for her chores. Or for not taking time to simply enjoy the day.

Now, she had too much time to do both.

The streets of Sugarcreek were busy. Kids were riding bikes and walking down the sidewalks. The ones from the English schools wore big backpacks heavy with textbooks. Mothers were walking with them, or window-shopping. Other men and women—both Amish and English—were darting in and out of buildings, obviously trying to get their errands done in an efficient way.

In the center of it all was the Grabers' store. Mrs. Graber was standing in the doorway talking to some customers. When Mary Kate drew near, the lady motioned her over just as the customers departed.

"Good day to you, Mary Kate. How was your day at the school?"

"Eventful," she replied with a smile.

"*Kinner* have a way of keeping things bright and busy for sure." She smiled, though the light didn't quite reach her eyes.

"Is everything all right?"

"Me? Oh, *jah*." After glancing into the doorway, she sat down on one of the rocking chairs that were displayed on the porch.

Mary Kate sat down, too. "Are you sure?"

"I apologize. It's just that . . . well, we're experiencing a bit of a hardship in our family. My daughter Judith just had a miscarriage, you see."

"I am truly sorry."

"Me, too," Mrs. Graber said with a sigh. "Usually, I wouldn't be mentioning such things, but I'm terribly worried about her." She looked at her more closely. "And, if you don't mind me saying so, there's something about you that makes me think that maybe you've experienced hardship a time or two."

"*Jah*. That is true. I've, ah, had my share of difficult times." Mary Kate didn't want to disclose what had happened to her in Millersburg. After all, she'd come to Sugarcreek to try to forget everything.

"Have your troubles passed?"

"For the most part." Mary Kate had a feeling Mrs. Graber was looking for a bit of reassurance, for a way to remind herself that the troubles her daughter was facing would one day soon pass onto happier times.

For herself, Judith's tragedy was a good reminder that she wasn't the only person with pain in her past. "Is there anything I can do to help?"

"What could you do?"

"Do you need help in the store? I could help out on the weekends if you're shorthanded."

"That's mighty kind of you, but I think we'll be all right. I've got a lot of *kinner*, you know. If we need help, I'll ask them to lend a hand. But I do thank you for the offer, Mary Kate."

After sharing a smile, they both stood up.

"Well, I suppose I'd best get back inside. But thank you for visiting with me, dear. I feel better now that I got some of my worries off my chest."

"I'm glad you trusted me. And don't worry, I won't mention this to a soul."

Mrs. Graber looked at her shrewdly. "I never imagined you would, child. To me, you seem like the kind of girl who can keep a secret. Come back soon, Mary Kate. It's just about caramel-apple season. Next time you stop by, we'll save one for you."

"Thank you. And don't forget to ask me to work if you need help."

"I won't. You reminded me that it's only right and good to ask for help. I sometimes forget that."

"I sometimes forget that, too," Mary Kate murmured to herself as she walked on. She felt lighter, too. It was amazing how offering to help another person was just what she needed to brighten her day.

She was still thinking about that when she noticed a few teenagers leaving the new ice cream store in town, The Sugarcreek Scoop. Making a decision, she walked in and ordered a cone.

Helping others definitely did brighten her day. But ice cream helped, too.

Miriam had never liked working on Saturdays.

Beyond her obvious difficulty with getting up

in the mornings, the Saturday morning crowd at the Sugarcreek Inn was rarely made up of locals or regulars. Instead, most of the customers were tourists, some who were eager to spend more than an hour enjoying a leisurely breakfast . . . and others who wanted their food as quickly as possible so they could explore Sugarcreek and shop. Miriam was constantly attempting to either encourage diners to depart a little faster . . . or to deliver food as quickly as a server at a fast-food restaurant.

The unevenness of it made her a little crazy.

However, to her consternation, she seemed to be the only one who minded the scattered weekend crowd. Mrs. Kent was always simply happy for the customers. And the other girls didn't much care who they waited on, as long as they left a decent tip.

As she went to take the order of a man sitting by himself at one of the back tables, she paused. He seemed to be nervous, twiddling his thumbs, and glancing around in an uneasy manner.

As she strode over to his booth, she found herself curious. He was Amish, but she'd certainly never seen him around town. Clean-shaven and blessed with slightly wavy light brown hair and matching eyes, his posture was what set him apart, at least by her estimation. He was straight and tall. Almost regal-like. Or like a soldier, she decided.

Yes, he had a certain way about him.

"Do you know what you'd like for breakfast?" she asked a little hesitantly once she approached his table.

He pointed to the most popular choice on the menu, the Sugarcreek Inn Special. "I'll take that."

"What kind of eggs and toast?"

As he told her and she wrote it all down, she couldn't help but notice that he was starting to look even more upset.

She liked to think that she could handle most anyone with ease. "Sir, are you all right?" she asked. "Is anything the matter?"

"What? Oh, *jah*. It's just that I was looking for someone I thought would be here."

Ah. Now it all made sense. "Did you need another menu? Or, would you like me to wait on your order?"

He looked like he was going to consider it for a time, but then abruptly shook his head. "I don't think so." His voice hardened. "I thought she would have walked by, but I guess I was wrong. I'll go ahead and eat now."

His anger, just brewing on the edge of his voice, brought back her slight sense of unease.

So much so, she was tempted to ask who he was looking for. But of course, that was none of her business. "I'll be right back with your breakfast."

He nodded before turning back to the window.

There was a story about this man, Miriam

decided as she walked back to the kitchen. She hoped the woman he was waiting for showed up soon. She'd love to see what kind of woman would have a man like him on pins and needles.

After delivering another table's breakfasts, the man's order was ready. She picked up his plate in the kitchen, then approached him again. When she was about halfway across the restaurant, he turned and watched her approach.

His lips curved slightly when she placed the plate in front of him. "This looks delicious."

She smiled back. "I hope you will enjoy it."

"I bet I will." When he caught her eye, his gaze warmed and some of his discontent seemed to lift. "What is your name?"

"My *nohma*?"

"*Jah*. I mean, you have no name badge."

"It's Miriam. I mean, I am Miriam."

"Miriam, thanks for your smile. You've made a difficult morning a whole lot better."

His direct stare brought her up a bit short. She was so used to being overlooked and, still smarting over Junior's visit, her self-confidence had reached a new low.

She should be feeling pleased that a man as handsome as he was showing her any interest.

But there was something about him that made her wary. And because of that, she stepped backward, nodded politely, then turned away. Perhaps she was being silly. Perhaps her imagination was working overtime. Maybe he was nothing unusual.

But there was something about him that felt that way.

She spent the next half hour taking orders, bringing checks, and refreshing coffees. All the while, the stranger by the window ate methodically, most of the time staring out at the groups of pedestrians walking by.

Every once in a while, he would glance her way. His gaze would turn piercing and she would feel a little flattered. Such vanity embarrassed her, but she supposed her reaction was only natural.

When he set his silverware down and leaned back, she checked in on him again. "I hope you enjoyed your breakfast?"

"It was *gut*."

Setting his check on the table, she said, "You pay up front."

"I'll do that. Thank you again, Miriam."

"You're welcome." Mainly for something to say, she said, "Maybe I'll see you again soon."

"Oh, I'll be back. I'm sure of that." He met her gaze. This time, there was no hint of a smile in his eyes. Instead, he looked at her intently, almost as if he knew a secret that she didn't.

Any pleasure she'd felt from his attention vanished. He was a bit too strange for her to feel comfortable around. Strange enough that she hoped he wouldn't return anytime soon. She had enough problems without wondering about his.

Chapter Eight ✗

After Miriam got off work at two in the afternoon, she gathered up the stack of magazines she'd picked up at the library and walked down Main Street to Mary Kate's tiny apartment above the old Ace Hardware store. It had closed six months ago.

When Miriam had first realized Mary Kate lived there, she'd commented that she would be a little afraid to live above a vacant store. In addition, the building was tucked away from everything. The easiest way to get to Mary Kate's apartment was to walk up the alley from Main. The alley was narrow and run-down.

Most folks in town figured that the alleyway was the reason the store hadn't done too well . . . and why no one had opened up another shop since.

Mary Kate had laughed at her suspicions, though, saying she liked the privacy.

After catching up for a few minutes, they sprawled on her floor, sipping Cokes and flipping through old issues of *Better Homes & Gardens*.

The two of them loved looking at the magazines, at photos of their dream kitchens, and reading the travel section of the magazine and imagining the kinds of adventures they could have one day.

Supposedly, they were looking at gardening and cooking ideas. What they were really doing, though, was relaxing after a long week.

"Aren't you so glad it's the weekend?" Mary Kate asked.

Thinking about Sunday's lunch, where she was going to have to find a way for them to sit with Junior Beiler, Miriam shrugged. "*Jah*. Though I really haven't had much of a weekend yet. I always work on Saturday mornings, remember?"

"Sorry. I'm just so glad to have a break from that classroom. Some days, it's all I can do not to start counting weeks until I get off for Christmas. I really need to get away."

"Come now, your school year only started a few weeks ago. And you told me you spent a few weeks in Indiana before you moved here." Mary Kate had gone to visit her married sister in Shipshewana, Indiana. They'd visited the famous flea market, and spent long, lazy afternoons piecing together a quilt. The idea of having such an amount of time to relax had made Miriam jealous.

"It wasn't long enough." Closing the magazine she was reading, Mary Kate sighed. "I don't even know if Christmas vacation is going to be a long enough break."

Miriam studied her friend, noticing for the first time that she was looking serious. "Teaching school can't be that bad. I thought you liked it. Most women would."

For a moment, Mary Kate looked like she was considering how to respond. "I like the *kinner*, but I am learning that teaching in a one-room schoolhouse is not where my heart lies. I always feel like it's not my calling. That there's something else that I should be doing, but it's just out of my reach." She paused before continuing. "Sometimes I've found myself looking out the windows of the schoolhouse and counting the hours until the end of the day with as much anticipation as the students."

Miriam winced. "That's not good."

"I know." Mary Kate's green eyes turned shadowed. "I wish I felt different about my job. I've been praying about it, too. Surely God wouldn't have blessed me with this job if he didn't want me to succeed, right?"

Miriam wasn't sure about that. Lately, she'd actually begun to stop looking toward God to answer all her questions. She was tired of all her unanswered prayers about His plans for her life.

"Well, the Scripture does say that we're supposed to give all our worries to him," she murmured. Then, feeling bad about feeling lost herself, she said, "Actually, I've been having a lot of those same thoughts about my job at the restaurant."

"Truly?"

Miriam nodded. "I've been working at the Sugarcreek Inn for five years now. Though I like most everything about it, sometimes I yearn for a break." Flipping the pages of the magazine some more, she added, "I just wish I had a long vacation to look forward to like you do."

"I could help you plan something. You should take some time off, too."

"I would, if I thought I could." But she couldn't, of course. Her cousin Amanda's wedding was coming up in November. Just the other day, her mother asked her to consider taking the whole week off for Amanda's wedding. Though it was hard, Miriam had stayed firm in her decision to work instead. If she took time off, she knew what would happen. She would become the wedding's worker bee, sewing this, organizing that.

Amanda would have been very appreciative, but Miriam also knew her efforts would be mostly overlooked in the midst of all the excitement.

After the wedding was over, the reception wagon had gone back to the rental company, and the food had been eaten, Miriam knew she would return to work no more rested than when she'd left.

And probably even a bit depressed, too. It was hard seeing so many of her friends and family find love, get engaged and married, all while she was waiting for the Lord to finally decide that it was her turn.

As she glanced at Mary Kate, she swallowed hard. Maybe the Lord had given her a real friend and she hadn't even seen what a blessing Mary Kate had become in her life. Mary Kate was her age and single, too.

For the first time in a long while, Miriam was able to simply hang out with a friend and not feel like a third wheel. That was how she usually felt with her friends who were married.

Flipping open another magazine, Mary Kate pointed to a vacation picture. In it, a pair of English girls were sitting on beach blankets next to a swimming pool. They were sipping iced tea and wore oversize sunglasses. "Look at this pair, Miriam. When the school year is over, I might go to Pinecraft." Brightening, she said, "You ought to come with me. Just think of how much fun we'd have at the beach!"

It did sound tempting. Sort of. "You're not afraid to go so far away?"

She shook her head. "Florida isn't that far away. Sometimes I don't even think it's far enough." Reaching out, she squeezed Miriam's hand. "Please think about coming with me. We could stay in a little condo on the beach. It would be *wunderbaar*."

"Maybe." But as she imagined staying in a vacation condo with her vivacious friend, Miriam wasn't so sure it would be the best time for her. Mary Kate was very pretty. Though she supposed she shouldn't worry about her vanity, sometimes Miriam feared she looked even plainer and chubbier when standing next to her lovely friend.

"Only maybe?" Her brows rose.

Not wanting to admit her private insecurities, Miriam said, "You sound as if you already know you will have a good time. Why is that? Do you have friends there?"

"No. I . . . I am just anxious to leave Ohio."

Anxious? Miriam's interest was piqued. "Why are you so anxious? You just got here!"

"No reason." Her shadows returned. "Well, there is a reason, but it's nothing that I want to talk about."

"Are you sure? I'm a good listener."

"I'm positive. Besides, I'd much rather talk about you."

"Me? There's nothing to say about me." Besides, she'd just been brushed off rather ungracefully. She wanted to know more about why Mary Kate would be so anxious to leave the area.

"Are you sure?" Pushing the magazine to one side, Mary Kate gazed at her with concern. "You forget that I know you pretty well. There's something going on, isn't there? Something happened and you're not happy."

Obviously, what Mary Kate said was true. She was still depressed and embarrassed about the mix-up with Junior. Plus, she was going to have to figure out how to convince Mary Kate to sit with Junior at lunch. Since getting to know her friend, she'd noticed a true hesitance to meet new people, especially men. That was strange since it was obvious every eligible man couldn't get enough of Mary Kate!

Of course, she wanted Mary Kate to be happy. And with time, she was sure she would be happy that Mary Kate and Junior had found happiness together. But so far, she wasn't having too good of a time pushing aside her jealousy.

"It's nothing." Noticing the time, Miriam closed her magazine, too. "I better get on home. I promised Mamm I'd help her do some baking for church."

Mary Kate picked up the stack of magazines. "Are you sure you don't mind walking these magazines back to the library?"

"Not at all. I'll take them over to the library right after work one day next week. I'm out of books."

"You read more than anyone I've ever met."

Miriam smiled. It was true she loved to read. She loved to imagine she was living an exciting life, filled with invitations and scores of men wanting to catch her attention. "You make that sound like a bad thing. Which, I might add, is not a good thing for a schoolteacher."

"I like to read," Mary Kate said weakly.

"Sometimes," Miriam teased.

Looking a bit embarrassed, she nodded.

"Sometimes is right. I like to read but I've always been better at math and science. If *kinner* only needed to learn arithmetic, my life would be much easier. But all this spelling and cursive and reading gets the best of me. I run out of patience too fast, I'm afraid."

"Then why did you take the job?"

"Because I had to." Lowering her voice, she added, "But I don't think I'm a very good teacher. And I'm also starting to worry that coming to Sugarcreek was the wrong decision."

Mary Kate sighed and gazed out the window. "Plus, I've got one little girl who needs a lot of help."

"What kind of help?"

"She needs a reading tutor. Maybe even just a reading buddy. You know, someone to help her gain confidence. To make things worse, her brother came up to school on Friday afternoon. We had a little conference about Kaylene and discussed what we should do to help her."

"What's wrong with that?"

"I don't know. I had the feeling that he didn't understand why I didn't have more ideas for how to help her." Sounding a bit defensive, she continued. "What that man doesn't understand is that I'm responsible for all the children, from my tiny first-graders to my older students getting ready to graduate from the eighth grade. There are only so many hours in the day, you know."

"Yes, I suppose so." Miriam felt sorry for the little girl. She was starting to get the feeling that Mary Kate had already given up on her. "If you get desperate, let me know. I'm sure I'd love to read with her."

Mary Kate's eyes widened. "Do you mean that?"

"Of course."

"Is there any way you would stop by the school this week? You could meet Kaylene and maybe sit with her for a few minutes? Oh, Miriam, if you could help this little girl, I'd be so grateful."

"All right," she replied, feeling a little stunned. "I'll stop by as soon as I can."

"Oh, *wunderbaar*! I'll send a note home and say that I've got a plan for her to get some special help. Her brother will be happy about that."

"I've never heard of a *bruder* caring so much about a little sister's schooling."

"*Jah*, it's curious, ain't so? Kaylene is the youngest of eight children, and the only one still in school. It's so sad, both of her parents have passed away. Anyway, you'd think that one of her older sisters would be the one who worried about school but it seems to be the brother who Kaylene relies on the most. He's the one who came to school to visit with me."

A small thread of worry began to form in her

stomach. That sounded suspiciously like how Junior was with his sister. And . . . wasn't one of Junior's sisters named Kaylene? "What is Kaylene's last name?"

"Beiler. Do you know the Beilers?"

"Oh, *jah*."

"Then you probably know Junior Beiler."

"I do, as a matter of fact."

New interest sparked in her eyes. "Do you know him well?"

"I've known him for years. We grew up together." Every word felt stuck in her throat as she mentally braced herself for Mary Kate to talk about how he had sparked her interest.

Mary Kate looked relieved. "Oh, *gut*. Maybe you can help me decide how to talk to him."

"Why would you need my help?" In spite of knowing better than to say such things, she added, "I'm surprised you aren't jumping at the chance to talk to Junior Beiler. He's so handsome. One of the most eligible bachelors in town, most would say."

"Oh, he's a handsome man, all right. I suppose some might think he would be quite a catch with his blond hair and blue eyes."

"You . . . You aren't interested in him?"

"Me? Not at all." Looking vaguely embarrassed, Mary Kate said, "I'm not interested in dating."

"Truly?"

"I have no desire to be courted ever again," she said without a trace of doubt in her voice.

"Why? Every woman I know around our age is either courting or hoping to be courting." *Or already married,* she thought about adding.

A shadow fell across Mary Kate's face, and she stood up, brushing off her skirts, seeming to want to end the conversation. "I . . . I had a bad experience once."

"What kind of bad experience? Did you get hurt?"

"*Nee.*" Mary Kate wouldn't look her in the eye.

Miriam was starting to understand her friend in a new way. "Mary Kate, did that experience make you wary about men? Did something happen?"

"I, ah, once dated a man who wasn't the type to take no for an answer. He was difficult to get away from." Looking beyond Miriam, out the window, Mary Kate murmured, "Sometimes I fear that even Sugarcreek isn't far enough away from him. That maybe I'll never be far enough away."

Miriam was confused, but finally was beginning to understand her friend's constant talk of getting away. "Do you think he might be looking for you now?"

"*Nee.* Well, I hope and pray not." She pursed her lips, then said, "When I broke things off, he didn't take it well. My parents didn't really understand either—he is the son of their best friends. That is why I took this teaching job in Sugarcreek. I was willing to do anything to get away. To have an excuse to leave him behind."

Miriam shook her head in wonder, torn between the desire to hug Mary Kate tight and pester her with a dozen questions.

Here, they'd been practically in each other's pockets since Mary Kate arrived but never had her friend hinted that she had just come out of such a scary situation. "I don't know what to say."

"There isn't anything to say." Her voice turned brisk. "I was in an uncomfortable situation but things are better now. Please just don't mention this to anyone."

"I won't." But as Mary Kate stared at her, a fresh wave of fear in her eyes, Miriam felt chilled. Was there more to her friend's story than she had shared?

"I had better go." Miriam was desperate to know more but could tell her friend was done sharing her secrets. Rather than chance her pushing her away, she thought she should head home and give Mary Kate some space.

"All right." Mary Kate walked to the door and held it open. "Thank you for listening to me. All this time, I've kept what happened to myself. I didn't want you to think differently about me, and I really didn't trust myself to even think about Will." She sighed. "But now that I've talked a little bit about what happened, I feel as if the biggest weight has been lifted from my shoulders. *Danke*."

"I didn't do anything."

"You did more than you know. You know, someone just yesterday told me that it was good to share one's burdens. Now I realize that was mighty good advice." With a fresh smile, she said, "See you tomorrow at *gmay*."

Miriam smiled, but as she slowly made her way down the rickety steps leading down from Mary Kate's apartment, she wondered how in the world she was going to get through church and keep two friendships.

Tomorrow at church she was going to have to let Junior sit with them after services. She was going to have to watch Junior flirt with Mary Kate . . . all while knowing that Mary Kate wanted nothing to do with him.

And of course, to make matters worse, she was going to have to hold her own wants and thoughts close to her heart. There was no way she could ever let Junior know how much she wished that she was the girl on his mind.

And no way could she ever let Mary Kate know that she was so glad she didn't like Junior.

It was a terribly awkward situation. And, it seemed that she had no one to blame for it but herself.

Walking down the sidewalks of Sugarcreek,

Miriam realized that Mary Kate had had a very good idea. She, too, needed a break from her life.

Suddenly, sitting on a beach in Florida, doing nothing more than watching the surf lap the beach, sounded like absolute bliss.

Chapter Nine ⨍

Three long days had passed since Judith had sat beside her husband at the doctor's office and discovered that life as she knew it was over.

It had felt like much longer, though. Each hour had lurched and hobbled by, passing painfully. Lingering far too long, almost as if each minute had wanted to sit a spell and make an already painful moment of time even more disappointing.

Alternating between her heart breaking and her temper flaring, Judith had stayed close to home, even pushing aside Ben's efforts to soothe.

She felt bad about her behavior, that she hadn't reached out to her husband and attempted to offer him any sort of support.

But even the thought of attempting to console him felt like too much effort.

Besides, she had no right to soothe and comfort, did she? She was the one with the problem. It was her fault that she couldn't bear children. Not Ben's.

Yesterday she'd barely gotten out of bed. But today Ben had insisted she get dressed and eat breakfast before he left to go work at her family's store.

An hour after he left, she discovered why he'd done so. Her mother had come knocking, her face a testament of concern, her eyes looking about Judith's home with a sharp expression. No doubt not missing a thing.

Judith had stood against the living room wall, her arms folded across her middle as her mother eyed the wooden floor that needed to be swept, the area rugs that needed to be shaken, and the counters and tabletops that needed to be dusted.

At last, her mother turned to her with a sigh. "Judith, dear, I wish you would have asked for some help. Gretta and Clara and I could have come over and helped you clean."

Having her two sisters-in-law over would have been terrible. Gretta and Joshua already had two children and were expecting their third. Clara's twin girls were almost two years old and adorable. Though Judith didn't begrudge them their happiness, at the moment it would have been too hard to watch.

"I didn't need them here, Mamm."

"They want to help, dear. And they could help you with the *haus*. . . ."

Judith couldn't care less about what her mother thought about the condition of the house. She hadn't invited her *mamm* over, and she was too old to be shaking in her boots about her lack of housekeeping efforts.

Her temper snapped. "Mamm, this is my home. I know it's a mess right now. But to be honest with you, I don't care."

After giving her a long, thoughtful look, her mother said, "Daughter, I promise, I did not come over here to be critical. I came over to ask you to think about taking a little break from your duties here."

"What are you talking about?" As far as Judith knew, she didn't have any duties—besides taking care of Ben and the house. Which she hadn't been doing.

"Daed and I would love for you to be home for a bit," her mother said with false brightness. "Anson and Toby and Maggie would love it, too."

Little by little, Judith was starting to realize that her mother's invitation hadn't been instigated by her poor housekeeping.

And Judith knew it had nothing to do with her smaller siblings missing her. Anson was eleven now and had time for only himself. Toby was nine and thought only about school. And Maggie? As much as Judith adored her little sister, everyone knew that Maggie's heart belonged to her adored brother-in-law, Ben.

So, what was the reason? Was Mamm merely worried . . . or had Ben asked her to come? "I can't move back home."

"I'm not asking you to move home. Just spend some time there."

"Because?"

"Because you need some help." Her mother's tone was matter-of-fact. Firm.

Judith arched an eyebrow. "I don't need any help. And I am just fine here."

Leading the way into the living room, her mother touched the top of the sofa like she was afraid the fabric would dirty her blue dress. "I don't think so. Please consider coming home for a week or two."

"Mamm, I could never go home for two weeks. And what about Ben? He needs me here." The moment she said the words, she felt the guilt overwhelm her. What she, her mother, and Ben all knew was that she hadn't been doing anything for Ben in the last two weeks since she'd miscarried. She certainly hadn't been cooking or cleaning.

"Ben is working so much at the store, I doubt he'll mind if you take some time to seek the comfort of home."

"But this is my home."

"Judith, you know what I mean."

Yes, she supposed she did. Ever so slowly, her mother's unannounced visit—and Ben's insistence that she dress—was starting to penetrate her haze of pain. "This isn't a spur-of-the-moment idea, is it?"

"I'm afraid not. Your father's been talking to Ben at the store."

"Does Ben want me to leave? Does he not want me here?" Though she tried to conceal it, panic set in. Was Ben mad at her because she couldn't seem to stop crying?

Terrible questions steamrolled and flashed in her head, faster and faster.

Did Ben want her to leave because she couldn't have children? Did he not want to be married to her anymore? What would she do if he no longer wanted her to be his wife?

The panic grew and strengthened. Gaining energy, hurting her ability to breathe.

Her mother gripped her shoulders hard, almost shaking her out of her stupor. "Judith, please. Please calm down, dear. You're upsetting yourself."

Her eyes welled with tears. "I'm not upsetting myself. I *am* upset."

"Oh, my sweet girl. I so hate to see you like this."

The tender endearment, so often said when Judith had been a little girl, brought forth a vulnerable response. "Mamm, I'm trying. I promise. I am just so sad."

Holding her hand between both of hers, her mother's gaze softened. "Judith, dear, listen to me good. Ben is not upset with you. He does not blame you. He does not want you to leave him. He is merely concerned about you being home alone. He doesn't think all this time by yourself is helping you heal."

Little by little, the words started to make sense. "Are you sure Ben isn't mad?"

"*Jah.* I am mighty sure! Judith, asking you to

come home for a bit was only a suggestion. It wasn't because I think you should cook and clean more. It wasn't because I think you should already be over this news. It's because we are all worried." Her voice lowered. "But I think coming home for a bit is a *gut* idea. Then you could rest and not try to keep up with everything that doesn't really matter."

"Like housework?" Judith asked dryly. With their big family, her mother had taken a clean and organized house very seriously.

"Like a lot of things." After squeezing Judith's hand once more, her mother walked over to the kitchen sink. There, dishes had piled up and had spilled onto the countertop. Across from the sink, the stove looked just as forlorn. A film of dust and grime coated the range.

As Judith looked at it all through her mother's eyes, she finally understood why Ben had been so worried.

Nothing was the way Judith usually kept things. From the time she'd been a little girl, she'd liked order. She'd always been the one to keep things in the kitchen and bathrooms clean and neat. She'd nagged everyone else in the house to be neater, too.

For her to have let everything go the way she had meant that something was truly wrong. "I know I haven't been taking care of things. I know I'm not acting like myself. But . . . I've had other things on my mind."

"I know, dear."

As if she hadn't heard her mother, Judith's voice grew stronger. "The things that I've been dealing with? They are important."

"I realize that," her mother said simply. But her voice was lilted, like she wanted to add so much more, but was holding her tongue instead.

Though her feet felt like they were full of lead, she joined her mother in the kitchen and halfheartedly picked up a dishrag. "Are you sure Ben isn't mad about the *haus*? Did he ask you to come over to make me fix everything?"

"There is nothing to fix, dear."

"There's me."

"Child, for whatever reason, Got has made a decision. It was out of your hands. It is out of Ben's hands, too. Now all he wants is for you to feel better. He is worried about you. We all are."

Her mother pulled the dishrag from her hands, and guided her to a chair. "No one is complaining about your housekeeping, daughter. Especially not your Ben. You know how smitten he is with you! Why, if you never mopped the floor again he wouldn't care. But I don't think it's good for you to be alone all day."

"Being around the kids and the rest of the family isn't going to make me happier."

"Are you sure about that?"

"I am mighty sure that being around Anson is not going to improve my mood, Muddah."

Her mother tried to frown, Judith could see that she really did. But after several seconds of trying, her frown eased into a lovely smile. "You might have a point about that. But, dear, I also think that dwelling on your loss isn't healthy for you."

"Mamm, it's not just that I lost my baby. That would be hard, and I would mourn, but I'm old enough to realize that sometimes the Lord has a reason for a baby not being born. It's the fact that I'm never going to have any *kinner* that has made me so terribly sad. I can hardly stand the thought of it." She lowered her voice. "And worse, I simply don't know what I'm going to do the rest of my life."

"Ben said you were going to visit another *doctah*."

"We are."

"Then, there might be hope."

"Yes, but I don't know."

"Perhaps the Lord wants you to help raise your siblings' *kinner*. Or maybe He feels that you and Ben are a perfect family on your own."

"I love my husband, but I don't know about that."

"Maybe one day you'll want to adopt then."

"I can't think about adoption. Not yet."

"If we can't plan your future, let's plan your day. What do you want to do?"

All she knew was that she didn't want to leave.

This was her house, her home. Plus, this was Ben's home, the one place where he had roots. Their life together here was finally giving him happy memories. There was no way she was going to do anything to cause him more pain, and she knew in her heart that moving out of their house—even for a very short amount of time—would do that.

"Mamm, I need to stay here. Ben needs to come home to me here. But . . ."

"Yes?"

"Maybe I could clean things up? Could you help me make supper and set things to rights?"

"Of course I will, dear. I want to help you in any way I can."

"*Danke*, Mamm."

"There's no reason to thank me. I simply want to see your smile again." Before Judith could reply to that, her mother eyed the messy kitchen with a critical eye. "My advice is that we start at the top and work our way down to the floor."

"In that case, I think I'll watch where I step." All of a sudden, a burst of laughter caught in her throat, surprising her. She looked at her mother in shock. "I didn't think that could happen. I didn't think I would be able to laugh about anything ever again."

"Never is a long time, dear. It's been often said, but it is always true." And with that, she handed Judith a washrag. "Wipe."

Chapter Ten ✗

For the first time in, well, forever, Miriam wished the church service would never end. Here inside the Yoders' metal barn, sitting in the middle of all her friends, she felt secure.

It was just warm enough inside to relax her muscles and encourage her mind to drift a bit. She'd listen to the preacher, think about the story or Bible verse he mentioned . . . then would give in to temptation and let her mind drift. She'd apply the verse to her life, or to something that happened in the past, and little by little, she'd feel even more filled with the Lord's will and happiness.

But all too soon, it did end and she was standing up and preparing to sit with Mary Kate and Junior during a lunch that was sure to be exciting for Junior, uncomfortable for Mary Kate, and excruciating for her.

After they filed out of the barn, Miriam spied Junior standing with three of his siblings. She noticed he kept glancing at the long line of people. She knew the exact moment when he recognized her and Mary Kate because his features tensed.

Beside her, Mary Kate tensed, too. "Are you sure we have to do this? I really don't want to sit with him."

"I thought you'd want to get to know Junior."

"He's Kaylene's brother. I've met him."

"Yes, but he wants to get to know you."

"Miriam—" Mary Kate looked like she'd just drunk sour milk. "I really would rather not. . . ."

"I mean he really wants to get to know you," Miriam said, hating every second of the conversation. But a promise was a promise. No matter how hard it was, she needed to convince Mary Kate to at least sit with them at lunch.

Brightening her voice, she continued. "I'm sorry, Mary Kate, but he asked me to set this up and I promised him I would."

"You could have told me about this yesterday."

"I should have. I don't know why it slipped my mind." She didn't want to admit that she'd been half-afraid Mary Kate wouldn't show up.

Oh, what a pickle. It was all Miriam could do to keep her expression easy and friendly. In truth, she felt more ill at ease than Mary Kate looked.

When Mary Kate looked Junior's way again, he smiled. She groaned under her breath.

Miriam grabbed her hand and gave it a little tug. "Let's go over to him and say hello. You'll like his sisters. Most everyone does."

"And then?"

"And then we'll eat and be done."

"I hope so." Mary Kate let herself be dragged, but to Miriam's dismay, she had the sort of look one wore to get a root canal.

"Please try to be friendly, Mary Kate," she whispered.

Narrowing her eyes, Mary Kate said, "He means something to you, doesn't he?"

"Who? Junior?"

"Of course, Junior," she practically hissed. "Why in the world did you agree to set him up with me if you like him?"

"I don't," she lied. There was no way she was going to let Mary Kate see that she'd been pining over a man for years who had no interest in her whatsoever. "I set this up because he's taken with you," she whispered back as they walked the last ten feet to meet the Beilers.

"But that doesn't—"

Miriam cut her off with a hard look. "It does. Now, please, be nice."

The little group of four parted to make room for them when they approached. "Hi, Miriam, Mary Kate," Junior said. "Mary Kate, this is Claire, Beverly, and Randall. Three of my siblings."

Mary Kate smiled. "Now I know five of you. It's nice to meet you all."

"You moved here in August, yes?" Claire asked.

"*Jah*. I moved here from Millersburg. So not too far away."

When she paused, they all leaned forward. Eager to hear what else she had to say. But instead of continuing, Mary Kate only stood quietly.

Claire's friendly smile turned a bit strained. "And are you enjoying Sugarcreek? And teaching school?"

"I am enjoying Sugarcreek, and my job is going well enough, I suppose. Soon we'll have Christmas break, then spring break. Then, at last, I'll have almost three months of vacation." Mary Kate gave her first genuine smile then, much to Miriam's relief—until she realized how awkward her friend sounded.

Certainly, Mary Kate didn't realize how uncaring she sounded to Kaylene's siblings? She glanced at Junior to see his reaction, hoping against hope that he hadn't caught the edge of relief in her voice. But as she'd feared, some of the light in his eyes dimmed.

"So, you enjoy vacations?" he asked.

"Oh, *jah*. Next summer, I'm hoping to go to Florida for a time." Smiling at Miriam, she added, "I'm hoping to get Miriam to come with me. I know we'd enjoy ourselves at the beach."

"Who wouldn't?" Beverly said. "Are you going to try to go to Pinecraft, too, Miriam?"

"That's a long time from now. It would be nice, but I'm not sure if I'll be able to. I might be needed at the restaurant. Or somewhere else."

"Summer is a busy time for me," Randall said. "The long days mean I have more time working construction."

The conversation continued. It was easy and

low-key. If Miriam hadn't been so worried about Mary Kate saying the right thing, and wondering what Junior thought about her, she would have enjoyed it a lot more.

As it was, however, she felt like she was on pins and needles. Waiting for something unfortunate to happen.

Around them, a lovely lunch had been set out and most folks had already started to dig into their meals.

Anxious to fulfill her promise, Miriam blurted, "Maybe we should eat before all the food is gone."

Randall grinned. "Miriam, that is a super idea. I'm starving. Let's lead the way." Gallantly, he waved her toward him. She had no choice but to walk by his side to the line of tables.

Sometimes the luncheons were served by the women of the hosting family. Today, the Yoders had opted to have a more casual setup. Miriam was glad of that. As they walked through the line, she chatted with Randall about his job and a few of their mutual friends.

On her other side, Beverly and Claire were making plans to put up some applesauce. Having a bit of experience with that, Miriam shared her preferences.

After that, it was easy to follow Randall and his sisters to an empty table by the back porch of the main house. After she took a seat, she looked behind her, certain to see Mary Kate and Junior bringing up the rear.

Now that they'd all met each other, Miriam felt a true sense of relief. At last her obligation to Junior was over.

But to her surprise, only Junior had returned to the table.

The girls and Randall looked just as confused.

"Where's Mary Kate?" she asked.

"She said she wasn't hungry," he murmured with a frown. "Miriam, she said to tell ya that she'll walk over to your *haus* later."

"I see."

"Do you? Because I sure don't."

Well, Junior was irritated. But what could she say that wouldn't either give away Mary Kate's secrets or make Junior feel worse than he already did?

When Junior still stood there, looking shell-shocked, Randall patted an empty chair. "Have a seat, *bruder*, so we can say prayers and give thanks for this meal. I'm so hungry I'm about to eat this plate."

Junior rolled his eyes but sat down.

After they bowed their heads in silent prayer, they dove into the sandwiches and pasta salad.

It was a delicious meal. As usual, Miriam enjoyed eating someone else's cooking. The girls and Randall seemed to feel the same way, hardly saying much between bites.

Junior, on the other hand, looked completely disinterested. He kept moving his pasta around his plate and staring off in the direction where Mary Kate must have left from.

"What happened, Miriam?" he asked after a few moments. "I thought you were going to set everything up."

She noticed that his tone was faintly accusing. Okay, maybe it *was* accusing. "I asked her to eat with us. I thought she was going through the line with you."

"The moment you walked away with Randall, she said she was going to leave. Where did she have to go?"

"I don't know. Maybe she had to go home?"

"You aren't sure?"

"No, I am not. She's my friend, not my responsibility." Now she had a feeling that she sounded irritated, too.

"Junior, it's not Miriam's fault that Mary Kate didn't want to stay for lunch," Claire said.

"It's likely she had papers to grade or something," Beverly said.

"I doubt it." Junior forked a bit of macaroni salad in his mouth.

"When I see her later, I'll ask her what happened," Miriam soothed. "I'm sure she has a good explanation."

"Maybe."

With a teasing wink in her direction, Randall

said, "At least we got Miriam to join us. Of the two, she's much easier to talk to."

"*Danke*," she said lightly as the girls agreed.

They continued chatting, chuckling about a couple of their mutual friends who had just returned from a poorly organized camping trip to the Hocking Hills. Everything that could have gone wrong did.

When Junior didn't join in, Miriam had had enough. Though she felt bad that Mary Kate hadn't wanted to stay, her departure certainly hadn't been Miriam's fault. Carefully, she folded her napkin and then stood up. "Um, I told my parents I'd leave with them today. I'd better go find them."

"If you feel like canning applesauce on Wednesday afternoon, stop over," Beverly said.

"*Danke*. I just might do that."

"See if Mary Kate can come, too," Junior ordered.

"I'll ask . . . but I'm not sure if she's much of a cook."

"Just ask, would you?"

Only Junior seemed to not realize he was being rude. While Randall scowled at his brother, Miriam knew it was time to leave.

Grabbing her plate and trash, she said goodbye, then walked over to her parents, who just happened to be looking at her like she was the best daughter in the whole world.

Sidling up to her, her mother said, "If you wanted to visit with Junior a little bit longer, we don't mind waiting, dear."

"I was ready to go."

"All right. But as soon as we get in the buggy, I want to hear all about what you two had to say to each other. Isn't this the most exciting thing, Miriam?"

Finally, she could reply to a question with complete honesty. "*Jah*. Very exciting." All in the worst way possible.

As her parents exchanged knowing looks, Miriam's spirits plummeted. How in the world was she going to tell them the truth? They would be so disappointed.

But if she didn't tell them, things were only bound to get worse.

Oh, how did everything turn into such a muddled-up mess?

Chapter Eleven ✗

Mary Kate swiped at her eyes yet again in irritation. When were things going to become easier?

She sure wished she knew.

For the last six months, she'd been merely reacting to everything that had been happening. She had been running from Will. She had been trying to learn to be a decent teacher even though she had no gift for working with children.

And now, she was literally trying to guard her heart. Leaving her family and friends in Millersburg had hurt. There, she'd been part of a big group of friends. And her family, too, of course.

Her social life had been busy and fun.

Leaving all of them without a word about where she was going had been hard. Now she missed them all terribly but was too afraid to reach out for their support.

And as it was becoming more and more apparent that she wasn't going to be happy in Sugarcreek, she was just as reluctant to make friends. All that would become of that was another painful transition.

Of course, she'd had a moment of weakness where Miriam was concerned, but Mary Kate didn't think it could be helped. Miriam was truly one of the nicest people ever. One had to actively try not to be her friend.

And Mary Kate just wasn't strong enough to live completely by herself.

Just keep living hour by hour, she coaxed herself. That's all you have to do. Stop worrying about the future. Just try to get through the day.

But instead of making herself feel better, her words only made her feel even more alone and in limbo. She swiped away a new crop of tears. Lifted her chin a bit.

And then noticed that Mrs. Graber was walking almost by her side. "Oh, hello, Mrs. Graber. I'm sorry, I didn't see you there."

Mrs. Graber looked her over. "That is not a problem. I fear I snuck up on you." She smiled. "So, did you enjoy the church service today?"

"I did. Did you?"

"Of course." She smiled. "I always enjoy church. Especially when I am not hosting it!"

Mary Kate chuckled in spite of her blue mood. "My mother always says the same thing. Hosting church is a lot of work." She looked behind them but didn't see anyone nearby. "Did the rest of your family not attend church?" She could have sworn she'd seen them, but maybe she had been mistaken.

"Oh, they were there. All of them except for Judith and Ben. Judith still isn't feeling well."

"I am sorry."

"Me, too." She shrugged, as if there was nothing she could say about it at the moment. "Anyway, sometimes I like to walk home by myself. It gives me time to think, you know. And it's a beautiful fall day."

With a bit of surprise, Mary Kate looked around and noticed that fall had come to the area without her noticing. Some of the trees had started to turn and the air was now cooler. "It is beautiful out."

Mrs. Graber looked her over more closely. "Now perhaps you could tell me why you are walking alone?"

"I just needed some time to think, too. But I am glad for your company."

Mrs. Graber chuckled. "I feel the same way. Sometimes it's nice to simply walk next to another person without feeling the need to say anything."

"Yes, you're right about that." With a bit of a surprise, she realized that there had been very few times in the past three years that she'd ever felt like she could be at ease.

For too long she'd been afraid of Will forcing his company on her. Then she had to fend off her mother's questions about why she was avoiding Will.

"Mrs. Graber, walking like this is nice, for sure. Thank you for joining me."

"We all need someone walking by our side, dear," she murmured. "I was happy to walk with you today—but please don't forget that the Lord is always with you, too. I've found it's nice to lean on Him a bit from time to time."

Mary Kate nodded, feeling soothed by Mrs. Graber's words. For too long she'd struggled to feel God's presence in her life. Now, she was so skittish, she was afraid she wouldn't notice His presence even if He were there. Maybe instead of trying to keep to herself so much, she needed to start trusting the One Whom she could really count on.

All day on Monday, Miriam struggled with the way Mary Kate had left them at lunch. Though she sympathized with Mary Kate's past and completely understood her reasons not to want to enter a relationship with Junior, Miriam didn't understand her friend's behavior.

She'd actually thought Mary Kate had been pretty rude to the whole Beiler family. And even if she wasn't interested in Junior, Mary Kate was new in town. Everyone could use some friends, right?

But instead of gritting her teeth and making the best of an awkward situation, Mary Kate had taken off without even saying good-bye and had really embarrassed Miriam.

Though she'd tried to temper her hurt and

anger, instead of easing as her Sunday passed, they only got worse. Mary Kate had told Junior that she would stop by Miriam's home later that day and explain herself.

So Miriam had spent the day avoiding conversations about Junior with her mother, biding her time until Mary Kate came over and they could discuss everything.

But Mary Kate never came.

That was when Miriam knew she was going to have to find an opportunity to talk to Mary Kate herself. She kept half waiting for Junior to show up unexpectedly, wanting a report on what Mary Kate had said.

She quickly walked over to the schoolhouse after work. But when she got there, the building was all locked up. One of the men in their church group was pulling some of the weeds in the pretty flower beds around the front walkway.

"Miss Mary Kate took off as soon as the last child left here," he said. "Scurried out of here like her feet were on fire, she did."

Miriam thanked him for the report, then turned around and walked all the way down the other side of Main Street. She was determined to put things to right with her girlfriend, no matter what.

She'd just passed the Grabers' store when she spied the man who'd been sitting alone in the restaurant the other day. He was walking toward her, and once again his gaze was piercing. He also looked mildly irritated.

She ducked her head as they got closer, hoping he wouldn't recognize her. But instead, he stopped and signaled to her.

"You're the woman from the Sugarcreek Inn, aren't you? You were my server."

"*Jah.*"

"Miriam."

"You remembered my name." She tried to sound happy about that, but in truth it made her feel a little uneasy.

"I never forget faces or names."

For some reason, she wasn't comforted by that statement. "That's quite a talent," she said lightly, hoping to merely share greetings then move on.

"I was just out for a walk this afternoon. Would you care to walk with me for a little bit?"

His invitation was too forward. And made her feel even more apprehensive to be around him. "I'm, ah, sorry, but I'm on my way to see a friend."

"Are you meeting your boyfriend?"

"*Nee*, it's a girlfriend." Then of course she wished she hadn't said anything. It was none of his business. And she was getting the feeling that the less he knew about her the better.

"So you don't have a boyfriend?"

His probing questions were starting to make her *naerfich*. "I must go."

"Of course. Don't worry, we'll see each other

again soon." She swallowed hard and started walking. His confidence unsettled her. She'd never met a man who'd been so forward. She didn't know what to think about him. She breathed a sigh of relief when she was sure he hadn't followed her.

Her heart beating a bit too fast, she stopped at the empty hardware store, raced upstairs to Mary Kate's apartment, then pounded on her door. When she heard nothing, she knocked even harder. "Mary Kate?" she called out. "Mary Kate, are you here?"

With a click of a deadbolt, Mary Kate opened up her door. "Whatever is wrong? You knocked so hard you could have woken the dead."

"Nothing's wrong, I simply wanted to see you. May I come in?"

Mary Kate stepped back to allow her in. The moment Miriam walked inside, Mary Kate shut the door behind her and clicked back the deadbolt.

Miriam looked at the thick lock on the door in surprise. "Why are you locking the door?"

"I always do. Now, why are you looking so flustered and out of breath?"

For a moment, Miriam was tempted to tell her about her encounter with the man from the restaurant and his personal questions. But on second thought, she pushed it back. Mary Kate was obviously feeling a little worried, and the last thing she needed to hear about was Miriam's suspicions about an unfamiliar man. Talk about letting her imagination get the best of her!

"I've been chasing you down all afternoon, since you didn't stop by my house yesterday."

Mary Kate's expression turned mulish. "Is that right? What do you need to talk about?"

"Yesterday's lunch, of course. I can't believe you left like you did."

Mary Kate crossed her arms in front of her chest. "So you came over to yell at me?"

"I came over to get a reason, since you didn't feel like telling anyone why you were so anxious to leave. And, for your information, I am not yelling."

"I had told you that I didn't want to eat with the Beilers."

"I know you said you weren't interested in Junior, but if you just got to know him . . ."

"I have nothing against Junior, Miriam."

"Well, you had to have known the way you left would make things awkward for me. Junior was pretty upset."

Mary Kate stared at her for long moment, then unfolded her arms and turned away to the window. "Miriam, I told you about what happened between me and Will. And I've told you about how I felt about my job at the school."

"And . . ."

"And, those two things seem like pretty good

reasons not to want to sit with a man who wants to date me and just happens to have a sister who is struggling in my classroom." She turned back to Miriam, her look vaguely accusing. "And, if you want to know the whole truth, I was irritated with you. You set up a date with me and Junior without even asking how I felt about it."

"It was hardly a date."

With obvious impatience, Mary Kate shrugged. "I'm sorry if I was rude, but all of it could have been avoided if you simply asked me if I wanted to sit with them instead of telling me."

"I told you, he really likes you. And he's such a *gut* man. You should give him a chance."

Mary Kate winced. "I can't. I simply cannot."

Miriam practically gaped at her. "I know you don't want to enter another bad relationship, but you have to realize . . . Junior Beiler, well, he's the most eligible bachelor in town! So many have wondered why he hasn't married yet, and here he finally takes an interest in you . . ."

"Miriam, I don't know how many ways I can tell you this. I am not interested in Junior. For your sake, I wish I was. But I'm not. At all."

Relief warred with frustration. Miriam hated to think of Mary Kate and Junior being together. But she also hated the idea of Junior pining for Mary Kate and continually using Miriam to get Mary Kate's attention.

"Is there something else going on?" Mary

Kate's tone was softer now. "Do you like him?"

"It doesn't matter if I did."

"Sure it does. We're friends."

"Mary Kate, Junior Beiler doesn't think of me in a romantic way." As much as it pained her to say the words, they did feel cleansing. Sometimes confronting the cold, hard truth made a person feel better. Kind of.

"Maybe he will one day." Her voice gentled. "He'd be a fool not to come to his senses and see that you're super."

"I doubt that."

"Miriam, as soon as the school year ends, I'm going to tell the school board that I don't want to return. I don't want to be a teacher anymore. I'm not good at it, and it's not fair that the children have to have someone like me as their teacher."

"I'm sure you're a better teacher than you think."

"Even if I am, I know I don't want to stay in Sugarcreek."

Just the thought of losing her best friend so suddenly made her feel sick. "There are lots of other things you can do here. Why, you can work at the Sugarcreek Inn with me."

"*Nee.* I want to leave. I need to leave. I really am hoping to move to Florida." Looking at her somewhat ramshackle apartment, she said, "I had hoped I would be happy here. Maybe even start over. But every night when I go to sleep my heart beats loudly. I get scared. It's not far enough away, Miriam."

"Why are you so scared? Have you heard from Will?"

"*Nee.* I mean, not exactly. There's just something inside me that feels a little strange. Every once in a while I feel a prickling at the back of my neck, like he's nearby." She shook her head, like she was clearing her head. "I'm sure it's just my imagination, though."

Mary Kate sounded so firm, so final, Miriam knew she wasn't going to change her mind.

And that made her more depressed than ever. At the end of the school year Mary Kate would be leaving. And Miriam would be remaining in Sugarcreek, doing the same job that she was tired of, living with her parents who wished she was living in another house as someone's wife.

Only now, it would be worse. Because her parents would think that Miriam had messed up her chances with Junior. And she would have no other single girl who was so like her to confide in and joke with.

She'd be more alone than ever.

That lump that had formed in her throat got a little bigger. It seemed she had misjudged a lot of things lately. She'd been so sure that one day Junior Beiler was going to look at her and suddenly return her affections.

She'd been so certain that she and Mary Kate were as close as sisters, that they'd built a strong friendship with each other, and it would always be that way.

Now it felt as if everything was spiraling even further out of control. No matter how hard she was attempting to hold on to her dreams, it was obvious that it was time to let them go.

Mary Kate sighed. "Miriam, please don't look so *bedrohwa*, so sad! I promise, none of this is your fault. If anything, you should be pleased about everything I've been saying. Obviously, I'm a mess! I've got a lot of problems right now. At the moment I'm not being a very good friend or teacher. And I'm certainly in no condition to be a good girlfriend."

"I hate to hear you say things like that."

"Sometimes the truth hurts, but it needs to be said. But I'm okay with that, too. I promise, Miriam, there's really nothing to be so upset about."

Miriam tried to push the thoughts of her friend leaving out of mind. For now, she had to deal with the issue at hand. "I wonder what I should say to Junior the next time we meet." Trying to lighten the tension and make a joke about her situation, Miriam looked at Mary Kate hopefully. "Any ideas?"

"I don't think it's your job to tell him anything," she said gently. "He shouldn't ask so much of you. And don't worry, if he asks me to go out with him next time I see him, I'll tell him how I feel."

"Don't do that!"

"Miriam, I don't like him. He seems like a perfectly nice person, but he's not the man for me. No man is right for me right now."

"I'll have to tell him something else."

"Miriam, he shouldn't have gotten you involved in the first place. We're not silly teenagers. If he wanted to get to know me, all he had to do was talk to me at school. You shouldn't feel so responsible."

"Easy for you to say."

With a sigh, Mary Kate crossed her arms over her chest. "Miriam, I think the real question is, what do *you* want to do about Junior Beiler?"

Ruthlessly, she pushed any and all visions of Junior gazing at her with affection away. Instead, she lifted her chin. "This conversation is not about me."

"But maybe it should be. Don'tcha think? And for the record, though he seems like a nice man, he doesn't seem all that special. If he doesn't already see what a good person you are, then you shouldn't waste another minute of your time on him. You deserve someone better."

Miriam supposed Mary Kate had a point. But that was because Mary Kate didn't know Junior like she did. "Let me tell you a story about Junior. When his *daed* died, he was barely twenty years old. Just a kid, really, just coming off his *rumspringa*. He loved sports, loved to hang out with his friends. He . . . He was just an average man, you know?"

"What happened when his *daed* died?"

"Just a few weeks after, a couple of their relatives who had stayed after the funeral made some offers. They wanted to break up his family. All the aunts and uncles were each going to take a couple of the siblings and raise them. They were very kind about it, of course. They wanted to help care for their nieces and nephews. But Junior refused to let any of them leave."

Mary Kate blinked. "Even Kaylene? She must have been very small then."

"She was only four. He was especially protective of Kaylene, and she was the one his relatives wanted to take most of all. One day I was working at the Sugarcreek Inn and I heard him arguing with some cousins from Pennsylvania. I didn't mean to eavesdrop, but their voices got loud. Anyway, I heard him say that he loved his sister, loved his family more than anything in the world. And that he would do anything he could to keep them all together. Even give up all his dreams."

Miriam sighed, getting slightly choked up at the memory. "That was when I knew he was a really special person, Mary Kate. I understand why you're not excited about being courted. But I will tell you that if you ever do change your mind, he would be worth it."

"I'll remember that, Miriam. Thank you. So, are we done arguing yet?"

"I'd like to be."

"Me, too." Gesturing toward her couch, Mary Kate asked, "Want to sit down and tell me about your day?"

"Only if you tell me about your day at school."

Mary Kate chuckled. "Something did happen today that was kind of cute. Little Sammy Yoder brought in a pig's tail today. And his pet lizard. Of course both got lost in the classroom." She rolled her eyes. "That lizard created quite a ruckus, I'll tell you that!"

Settling into the soft cushions of the couch, Miriam said, "That sounds a lot more fun than making five chicken potpies and waiting on a table of six who didn't believe in tipping. Although . . . Mrs. Kent has an admirer."

"Who?"

"The new manager of the English grocery store! He came over to the restaurant just to see her."

And just like that, they were chatting like they used to. Sharing stories and commiserating about the life of being working girls.

After another hour, Miriam went home feeling a hundred percent better.

She'd needed that girl time.

In fact, she was feeling so good about things,

she hardly minded her mother grilling her about her day, and whether she had any plans with Junior.

She was just about to admit the whole ugly truth about Junior and his infatuation with the uninterested Mary Kate when her father opened the front door and called for her.

Concerned, Miriam rushed from the kitchen to see what he needed. "Yes, Daed?"

"Looks like your young man has returned, Miriam."

While she could practically feel her mother beaming behind her, she said, "Daed, what are you talking about?"

"Junior Beiler is at the end of the street, walking toward here with a spring in his step. Looks like you've got a caller tonight, dear."

Her mother clasped her hands together in what looked like a combination of excitement and prayer. "Oh, my goodness." Then she looked at Miriam and frowned. "Miriam, go freshen up!"

At the moment Miriam didn't care whether she looked fresh or not. But she definitely did need a moment to gather her thoughts, so she rushed to her room and washed her face.

And took the time to pray. *Lord, I don't know what you have in mind for me tonight, but please stay with me, would you? I think I'm going to really need you more than ever.*

Almost as soon as she finished her brief,

somewhat frantic prayer, her mother called out for her.

"Miriam, do you want to serve cheese and crackers or yesterday's brownies?"

If Miriam had been the type of woman to stomp her foot in frustration, she definitely would have. For the first time in her life, she was dreading a chance to chat with Junior Beiler.

"Neither," she grumbled as she walked down the stairs.

Chapter Twelve ✗

The moment Miriam left, Mary Kate turned both locks on her door, then pulled out the letter she'd been reading when Miriam showed up unannounced. Though she'd meant to keep her whereabouts a secret, she'd given into loneliness and had reached out to her parents.

Slowly she sat down on the couch, carefully unfolded her mother's letter and steeled herself to read it yet again.

However, it didn't matter how much she tried to remain calm. Within seconds, her pulse began to race and her hands began to shake as she forced herself to read the words for a third time.

Last night, we had dinner with the Lotts and just happened to see that nice Will. He's gotten so handsome, Mary Kate! And he's so considerate, too. He sat down with us, asked about my sprained wrist (more about that later!), and then said he couldn't leave without hearing all the latest news about you.

Even though you asked me to keep it a secret, I simply had to tell him all about how you're a teacher.

He was mighty surprised!

But then he said he thought you must be a

good one, because you are so smart and sweet. Dear, he also asked me to be sure you knew that he was thinking about you.

Wasn't that so kind of him?

I don't know what happened between the two of you, but I hope you forgive him soon. You know how all of us have hoped and prayed that you and Will would one day marry.

Her mother's note continued, telling Mary Kate about how she tripped on her father's boot that he'd left out in the middle of the room in the middle of the night. She told her all about going to the doctor to get her wrist looked at, but how it wasn't broken but only a sprain.

More pages told about all kinds of things, none of which Mary Kate would ever remember.

All she cared about was that Will knew that she was teaching school at an Amish schoolhouse. Deep down, she knew it was now only a matter of time before he found her.

She knew she hadn't moved far enough away. She also knew that she wasn't going to be able to wait until June to head south.

Sometimes, it felt like Sugarcreek, Ohio, was just too small. No matter how hard Junior tried, everything he did was observed and commented upon by just about everyone he knew.

On the way over to Miriam's, he'd been

stopped by no less than four people asking what he was up to. It had taken some pretty impressive conversational somersaults to avoid telling the truth.

He had enough going on in his life without everyone giving him their opinions, too.

"Hi, Junior," Mr. Zehr called out from the middle of his flower beds. "Couldn't stay away, huh?"

"*Nee*," he mumbled, feeling vaguely foolish. Miriam's father had spoken so loud, the whole street probably knew he had stopped over again.

To make matters worse, the man waved, then walked right inside his front door. It closed with a snap behind him.

Hmm. That was strange. Unbidden, he heard Joe's words ring in his head as he walked the last hundred feet to Miriam's home. *You shouldn't go. It's not a* gut *idea.*

But recently, it seemed that he'd been in no hurry to listen to anyone's good idea. Which was why he was calling on Miriam again.

And, for some reason, he was feeling a little nervous.

Eager to take his mind off his worries, he tried to focus on her house. An old cottage-style home, built in the 1950s, Miriam's *haus* was tucked away at the end of a cul-de-sac on one of the oldest streets in Sugarcreek. Parts of the street were still made of brick, making it look charming and as if you'd stepped into another time.

It was clear Mr. Zehr spent a lot of time in his flower beds as an abundance of flowers decorated the yard. A trio of rocking chairs rested on the front porch, their shiny white paint standing bright under the green ferns nestled in hanging baskets.

Everything about the home spoke to the care of the details.

Just as he raised his hand to knock on the door, it opened, bringing him face-to-face with her mother. Deanna Zehr was a slightly older version of her daughter. She was a little heavier than Miriam, her skin a bit more lined and wrinkled.

But her eyes were just as bright, the dark blue looking almost black in the fading afternoon light.

"Hello again, Junior," she said. "We're mighty glad you've returned."

He felt lower than low. He had a feeling that he'd misled more people than just Miriam. "*Jah.* Hello to you, too. I, ah, came over to see Miriam."

"Oh, we know that." She looked absolutely delighted. "Lukas just told her you were walking down the street. She went to go freshen up. But she'll be back down soon. You know Miriam, she's not one to fuss too much."

He had three sisters, two of whom fussed a lot.

But they only fussed when they were interested in a boy. Beverly had taken to pinching her cheeks every time she was within two yards of Joe.

He clasped his hands behind his back and tried to look more at ease than he felt. "Ah."

"Did you enjoy yesterday's service at the Yoders'?"

"*Jah*. Very much so."

After another searching look at him, she nodded. "That is *gut*. So, um, how is your family?"

"They are doing well."

"*Gut*. Well, I suppose you would like to come in?"

"I would. I mean, if that is all right. . . ."

He was just about to step inside when Miriam appeared at the door. "I'll speak with Junior out on the front porch, Mamm."

"You sure? It feels a bit chilly."

"We'll be fine."

Her mother raised her brows, but only gave him a half-hearted wave. "I'll be seeing you, then, Junior."

"Good-bye, Mrs. Zehr."

The moment she was out of sight, Miriam shut the front door. Then she turned to him, her eyes anxious. "I'm sorry. My mother has started to become a bit too interested in my personal life. Do you mind sitting on the front porch? We'll have more privacy out here than inside."

"I would prefer that, actually." After they each sat down in one of the rocking chairs, he decided to get straight to the point. "Did you get a chance to talk to Mary Kate about why she left on Sunday?"

"I did."

"And?" He knew he sounded anxious, but he was curious to find out what had happened. "Why did she leave so suddenly? Did I do or say something that she didn't like?"

"Not at all." Looking perplexed, Miriam leaned back, allowing her chair to push her forward and back. "Why would you think you said or did something wrong?"

"I don't know." Pulling off his hat, he wiped his brow that had suddenly started to perspire. "It just seemed strange that she rushed off like that. What was Mary Kate's reason?"

"A couple of things . . . she, uh, had some work to complete and some chores to do before school today."

"That was her reason?"

For a moment, it looked like she wasn't going to answer him, then she nodded. "*Jah*. Um, Mary Kate can be a little thoughtless sometimes, I fear."

"And why is that?"

"She is, um, having some personal problems."

"What kind of problems?"

She hedged. "Junior, I don't know if I should

tell you. Her story really isn't mine to tell, you know?"

"I hear you. But, Miriam, you've got to help me out at least a little. I feel like I'm forcing her to talk to me against her will, and I don't know why she's acting like that. Most people like to talk to me just fine."

"What's going on isn't your fault."

"What is going on?" His voice was more plaintive now. "Please tell me. I need some help. I never thought I'd be the type of man to act like this."

Miriam swallowed hard, looked beyond him, then seemed to come to a decision. "She was in a bad relationship before she moved to Sugarcreek. Toward the end, she had begun to be afraid of that man."

He felt like he'd just swallowed an ice cube. "Did he hurt her?"

"No. I mean, I don't think he did. But she's wary of men now."

"She's afraid." All of his protective instincts rushed forward and, if anything, his feelings for her strengthened. Mary Kate was such a little thing. Tiny. It boggled his mind to imagine another man hurting her.

"Miriam, I don't know what to say. I never expected anything like this."

She smiled softly. "I know what you mean. I was shocked when I heard her story, too." She paused. "But maybe knowing some of her history? Maybe it will help you understand her a bit better."

"It does. It really does." He shifted, knowing it was probably time to go, but the sun was shining on their shoulders, Miriam seemed more relaxed, and for the first time all day he felt at ease. "Miriam, why do you think we never talked very much before now?"

Something flashed in her eyes before she shrugged. "Oh, gosh. I don't know. I guess we were both too busy."

"Maybe. For the last four years, all I've been doing is trying to keep up with my siblings. Trying to make everything all right for them."

"And I've been working," she allowed. "Sometimes working far too much. It's hard to do things with friends when you are always tired."

He laughed. "I know what you mean. When our *daed* first died, Levi had a couple of months of bad dreams. He kept dreaming that someone else would die and he'd have to go live with other relatives."

"That poor boy."

Junior smiled softly. "I know. He was afraid my other brothers would laugh at him, so he crawled into my bed every night, even though he was twelve years old! He'd crawl in, then toss and turn. Kick in his sleep." He winced at the memory. "It about broke my heart, if you want to know the truth. Next thing I knew, I'd be wide awake. And then there was nothing to do but stay by his side and watch over him. Which meant, of course, that I'd be exhausted the whole next day."

"So, that's what you've been doing all this time, Junior. You've been trying to be a mother and father to your siblings." She grinned. "And trying to get some sleep."

"Those days are just about over now. I wouldn't be surprised if Beverly got married soon. Randall, too. And Claire, Neil, and Micah are self-sufficient now. Levi is on the verge of being that way. So all that is left to worry about is Kaylene."

Junior paused. While he knew how much he focused on his family and making sure everyone had what they needed, he never realized why he'd been pursuing Mary Kate. Deep down, as pretty as she was, he also thought that someone that Kaylene already knew, like her school-teacher, would allow him to build a little family for his sister. Make sure she had a place to live where she felt like she belonged. Of course, it hadn't worked out the way he imagined. Mary Kate was standoffish, and Kaylene didn't seem to take to Mary Kate the way he'd expected her to.

Junior leaned back in his chair and sighed. "I had thought finding the right partner was going to be so easy. That once I'd decided I had time to date, I'd find the right girl, go courting, and get married. But I'm finding out that it's not that easy."

She smiled softly. "That doesn't surprise me."

He didn't know why he was confiding so much to Miriam, but sitting here in the late afternoon on her porch, it felt like he could finally open up about things that he usually kept to himself. Lowering his voice, he said, "The truth is, I don't think Kaylene likes Mary Kate all that much."

"No?" She paused, seeming to search for the right words. "Well, to be honest, I think Mary Kate is a wonderful person and a good friend. But I don't believe that she loves teaching school." She shrugged. "And it could be that Kaylene's struggles make Mary Kate frustrated, like she knows she's not doing a good job."

"*Jah.*" Miriam's words were wise. She seemed to truly understand the situation.

He looked over at her, hoping to catch her eye and share a smile of gratitude. Despite what he'd thought for so long, she no longer seemed too introverted and shy. Instead, he found himself thinking how easy she was to talk to. How comfortable she was to be around.

Instead of thinking she wasn't perfectly beautiful, he noticed those blue eyes of hers, that they were not only striking but incredibly telling. With one quick glance, he could discern everything she was thinking.

All this time, he'd been missing out on getting to know her better. All this time, he'd been missing out on having a friend like her.

Feeling weary, he got to his feet. "I had better get on home. Thanks for talking with me."

"Anytime, Junior. I enjoyed it."

He smiled at her before turning and walking back to his house. But as he started his walk, he realized that Miriam had been sincere in her offer.

He knew, deep in his heart, that she would talk to him anytime that he asked her to. She was that type of person, completely unselfish that way.

What was more surprising was that he'd known that for some time. Though he'd practically ignored her for most of their lives, he'd thought nothing of asking her for help to get Mary Kate's attention. He'd known he could trust her.

And though it was obvious that she'd thought he'd come calling for a different reason, she'd agreed to help him without hesitation.

Tonight he'd done the same thing again, badgering her for information, asking her for help. And yet again, she'd given him what he'd wanted freely and without expecting anything.

And he'd taken everything she'd given with a throwaway smile and the briefest of thanks.

As he turned the corner and headed toward home, Junior realized that he'd gotten a lot of information that evening. Some of it was about Mary Kate—but far more of it had been about himself.

He really had been trying to parent his siblings. He really had put his needs last for the last several years. Because of that, he'd been tired. And a little overworked. And a bit stressed.

But he didn't regret a single moment. He was proud of his siblings. And proud that he could honestly say that he'd done the best he could.

And that was something his parents would have been very pleased about, too.

Chapter Thirteen ƒ

"Judith! Look at you!" her father called out from the back of the store.

Of course, his voice reverberated through the aisles of the crowded store like a bullhorn, signaling anyone and everyone to stop what they were doing and stare at her.

She could have killed him.

It was just after lunch and she'd gathered the energy to walk to the store to surprise Ben. But having all these strangers surrounding her was making her nervous.

She was about to bolt out the door when she saw Ben approach, a huge smile on his face.

"Hiya, love. What a nice surprise! I'm going to go tell Daed that you and I are going for a little walk."

She reached out and grabbed his sleeve. "You can't go anywhere. The store is packed."

"He can handle it."

She knew he was bluffing, though. When the store was as crowded as this, every Graber needed to be on hand. She was trying to get up the courage to tell him to stay when she felt a firm hand on her elbow.

"Ben, how about I take your wife out for ice cream?" Miriam Zehr asked.

Judith could see the look of relief on his face, but he turned to her first. "Is that all right with you?"

"It is fine," she murmured. She would have said anything to help him out. But to her surprise, the thought of spending some time with Miriam did feel fine.

Once outside, Judith stopped and breathed deeply. "Miriam, you have perfect timing. *Danke*."

"Of course. Have you been to the Sugarcreek Scoop yet? The ice cream there is *gut*."

"I haven't had a chance to go yet."

"It's time you went, then." Miriam started walking at a brisk pace. Judith wondered if she was anxious to get to the ice cream shop or if she was trying to get Judith away from the store.

While Judith concentrated on keeping up, she tried to recall the last time she and Miriam had chatted. Gretta had worked closely with Miriam at the Sugarcreek Inn for years. And since Joshua had courted Gretta forever, their paths had crossed many a time. Miriam was also good friends with Lilly Miller, who had been their next door neighbor for a time.

Miriam glanced over her shoulder and bit her lip. "Are you okay? Am I walking too fast?"

"Not at all. I was just thinking about our connection. How you worked with Gretta and Lilly."

"We seem to all be connected one way or another here in Sugarcreek," Miriam agreed with a shy smile. After they crossed one block, the new store's sign loomed. "Here we are."

They went into the brightly painted shop and both ordered ice cream sundaes. Then, because the day was so nice, they elected to sit outside at one of the shiny white tables arranged on the side of the building.

Judith hadn't had any appetite to speak of, but that first bite of caramel topping and dark chocolate ice cream tasted heavenly. "This is so good."

Miriam lifted her spoon filled with vanilla ice cream and hot fudge sauce. "I agree." With a pleased smile, she took another bite. "It's a treat, for sure."

"So, what have you been up to? It's been a while since we've talked." Judith didn't want to state the obvious . . . that she'd been avoiding church and all social gatherings since the miscarriage.

"Me? Oh, nothing too much. Working at the inn."

"How are things at the restaurant?"

"They're good enough, I suppose. How are you? I heard about your miscarriage. I am sorry, Judith."

Judith looked at her in surprise, shocked at how matter-of-fact Miriam sounded. "*Danke.* It's

hard, but with God's help, things will get better."
Eventually.

"You are right about that, about Got helping us through each difficult moment. Sometimes I forget that."

"Lately, I have too." And that shames me, Judith silently added.

Miriam studied her face, looked at her dish of ice cream, then, to Judith's surprise, pushed it away. "Lately, I've been feeling like nothing is going right for me. I'm tired of being a waitress. Even more, I'm kind of tired of waiting and hoping for some man to fall in love with me."

Judith didn't dare offer a platitude. She'd heard enough of those over the last few days to fill up a kitchen sink. Instead, she offered a question. "Do you have someone in mind?"

"*Jah*. But he doesn't feel the same way."

"I'm sorry."

Miriam shrugged. "I know my problems don't compare to your loss, Judith. I don't mean to sound like I think they do. But even so . . . I kind of have a constant pain in my heart. It's hard, hoping things will eventually change . . . but then they just stay the same."

Judith looked at her ice cream bowl. To her surprise, she'd eaten half her sundae. Now that it was half-melted, she pushed it away, too. Then looked at Miriam.

Miriam had made Judith remember that they

all had their share of struggles to bear. While she was longing for children, Miriam was still longing to find love and companionship in her life. It made Judith thankful for the blessings she did have, namely a man like Ben.

With that in mind, she reached out and gently squeezed Miriam's hand. "*Danke*. Thank you for sitting here with me. For reaching out. You made my day better."

Miriam waved an embarrassed hand. "Judith, I've been sitting here telling you my problems!"

"*Jah*, but they're important, too."

Miriam smiled. "I have a feeling we'll both get through this rough time with the Lord's help . . . and a whole lot of hope."

"Indeed." And with that, Judith picked up her spoon and took another bite. It would be a shame for all that chocolate and caramel to go to waste, after all.

After she said good-bye to Miriam, Judith walked back to the store, where Ben was waiting for her on the front porch. Though he was leaning indolently against the front wall, his eyes were sharp. "You look better."

She had to smile. Leave it to her husband to get right to the point. "Actually, I feel better." She shook her head in wonder. "That Miriam has a way about her. We've hardly said much to each other in weeks—our paths just don't cross all that much—but now, talking to her? It felt like she was my best friend in the world."

"If she made you feel better, she's my new best friend, too." He winked as he walked down the front steps to meet her.

She stepped to his side, happy to have the twenty-minute walk home, just long enough to stretch their legs.

After they'd gone about halfway, he spoke. "Judith, I think we could use a little vacation. Why don't you do some thinking about where you'd like to go?"

"We don't need a vacation."

"I know, but it might be nice to get away." He brightened. "We could go out west. Colorado might be fun. Remember how we always talked about seeing Pikes Peak? We could do one of those Pioneer Bus trips."

"All right. I'll look into that." But Judith already knew she wouldn't. She didn't want to go away; she wanted to reclaim herself and her life. And she could only do that right there in Sugarcreek.

"Well, even if we don't take a vacation, I think we should go spend a few days at your parents' *haus*."

Judith frowned. "I already told Mamm I didn't want to leave you."

"I said *we,* Judith."

"You want to stay there, too?"

"Uh-huh." Looking sheepish, he said, "I'm sorry, but I could use a little bit of your family's craziness right about now."

"Anson *will* drive you crazy. Probably within ten minutes of our arrival."

He chuckled. "Maybe. But my little Maggie will make up for his peskiness."

"My little sister has you wrapped around her pinky."

Ben smiled. "That's no secret."

Judith pondered the idea of going to her parents' house while they walked another block. Looked at the terra-cotta pots filled with bright purple mums in front of one person's bungalow.

And watched a trio of schoolchildren chasing one another in their front yard. They were Englischers, but their antics were as familiar as some of her memories from growing up.

By the time they'd stepped onto their front porch, Judith knew that Ben's idea was the right one. "All right, then. Tomorrow at work, tell Daed that we're going to come stay for a while."

He smiled. "I'm glad you changed your mind. I'll tell him that we'll head over tomorrow evening. Okay?"

"Okay."

"*Gut.* Now come here and hug me, *frau.* I love you."

Stepping into his embrace, Judith closed her

eyes and gave thanks once again for her husband. Ben knew her so well. He spoiled her and always put her first.

And . . . sometimes he even knew when to ignore everything she said and take charge.

"I love you, too, Ben."

"I know," he whispered, pressed his lips to her neck. "I promise, I know."

Chapter Fourteen

No matter what might be going on in her personal life, Miriam was eager to lend her help to Kaylene Beiler.

From the moment Mary Kate had told her about Kaylene's struggles, Miriam knew that she would be willing to do anything to help the little girl. She had never had a difficult time in school, but she could only imagine how difficult it would be for a tenderhearted young girl.

She knew from experience what it felt like to be teased mercilessly when one was a little different, after all.

When Miriam walked inside the old white-washed schoolhouse, the smells of glue and crayons and pencils surrounded her . . . as did the stuffy scent of kids and tennis shoes and grass and snacks.

It felt like taking a giant step back in time.

Even if she'd been led into the building blindfolded, she knew she would recognize the place in an instant. Childhood memories were very strong, she supposed.

A glance at the chalkboard brought back memories of standing at the front of the class, solving sums. The rag rug by the windows reminded her of the stories Miss Hannah used to tell. The rows of neatly lined desks? Sitting behind Judith Graber . . . and mooning over Junior Beiler, who sat one row up and two rows over.

Mary Kate was chatting with Kaylene at the front of the room. And since they looked to be deep in conversation, Miriam took her time walking to the front of the room. With a smile, she read the bulletin board, filled with all kinds of information about assignments and activities that were planned.

Oh, but it all sounded so familiar!

Picking up a few dropped pencils, she noticed an overflowing pencil sharpener. Pencil shavings littered the counter and the floor around it. Unable to help herself, she carefully emptied it and then set it back in place.

Then straightened a stack of books. And gathered up a pile of papers, neatly fastening them with a paper clip she found next to a pile of chalk.

"Miriam, you shouldn't be cleaning the classroom," Mary Kate called out.

"I don't mind. It's giving me something to do." Meeting Kaylene's gaze, she said, "I don't want to disturb you two."

"You didn't disturb us; you're the reason Kaylene is here, right, Kaylene?"

Looking at Miriam warily, the little girl gave a little nod.

Mary Kate smiled. "I was anxious for you to meet Kaylene. Or have you met?"

"Well, we haven't spent much time together, but we do know each other, don't we?" Miriam said gently. "Kaylene, I want you to know that I'm looking forward to helping you as much as I can. I love to read."

Kaylene bit her lip, looking a bit embarrassed.

Mary Kate placed a comforting hand on the girl's shoulder. "All we're doing is trying to help you read better."

"*Jah.* I'm going to try my best to catch you up to speed."

"I don't know why I can't read good."

"Remember what we talked about?" Mary Kate said gently. "Everyone in the class has something they're good at and something that they need to work on. You simply need a bit of help reading."

The little girl nodded, but she looked sadder than ever.

Miriam decided to take things into her own hands. Picking up the two books Mary Kate had put aside, she said, "Let's go sit outside."

"Is that okay, Teacher?"

"Of course."

The moment they got outside, Miriam smiled. "This is better, don'tcha think? It's nice to be out in the fresh air. I don't know about you, but I would be ready to get out of that stuffy class-room by three o'clock every day."

Kaylene's eyes widened and she giggled a bit.

Feeling encouraged, Miriam pointed to a picnic table off to the side, near a pair of teeter-totters. "Want to go sit over there?"

Kaylene nodded.

When they got settled, Miriam looked at the two readers Mary Kate had picked out for them to work on. Both looked like beginning reader books. And both would probably help Kaylene.

But Miriam thought they also might embarrass her, too. She remembered reading the same stories when she first started school. They were a bit childish for an eight-year-old.

Instinctively, she knew that Kaylene was going to have to feel good about what she was reading in order to give it her best effort. With that in mind, she made a quick decision. She set the two books to one side, opened up her tote bag, and pulled out the book she'd picked up on a whim at the library right before she came to the school.

"Kaylene, have you ever heard of this book? It's called *Little Women*." Miriam had always loved the story. She'd loved Jo and the setting, and, of course, she'd liked the idea of being one of four sisters. She'd always wanted to have siblings her age.

Kaylene looked at the book with obvious skepticism. "What's it about?"

"It's all about four sisters who live in the 1800s during the Civil War."

Kaylene wrinkled her nose.

Miriam laughed. "I promise, it's a *gut* book. A mighty *gut buch*. The girls have all sorts of adventures. Since you have a lot of siblings, I have a feeling you might be able to relate to them."

"I do have a mighty big family."

"Well, I'm only one of three, and my brother and sister are much older."

Kaylene blinked, a new interest appearing in her eyes. "That's like me! I'm the baby of the family."

"Even Levi is much older than you, ain't so?"

"Uh-huh. He's eight years older. Levi is sixteen."

"I'm glad we have something in common then." Fingering the book cover, she looked at Kaylene. "So, would you like to give this a try? Or, we can read one of the books your teacher gave us. I promise, either is fine with me."

Kaylene glanced at the two readers, then at *Little Women*. "Let's read this, Miriam. I mean, if I can."

Miriam's heart went out to her. Instead of sounding excited about the story, she sounded almost as if she were getting punished.

Remembering that Mary Kate said Kaylene needed to work on both comprehension and her reading, Miriam said, "How about I read a paragraph, then you read one? Then, after we each read, we'll talk about what happened." After

Kaylene nodded, Miriam opened up the book. "I'll begin." She took a breath and started reading about a Christmas long ago, the coldest and snowiest one in memory.

After she read a few short paragraphs, she patiently helped Kaylene read out loud her section. After a few stumbles, Kaylene began to read more fluidly, and Miriam started to wonder if the little girl had simply needed a bit more confidence.

When Kaylene finished reading, they talked about what they'd read, Kaylene understanding far more than Miriam had expected her to.

When they went back to the story, Kaylene leaned a little closer to Miriam and the book. After they read five pages, she glanced at Miriam shyly. "I like this story."

"That makes me *verra* happy. Let's read a little bit more."

They'd just finished their tenth page when Kaylene looked up and burst into a bright smile. "We're reading!"

Miriam wrapped an arm around Kaylene's shoulders and gave her a little squeeze. "Indeed we are. I'm mighty proud of you!"

Kaylene looked like she was going to add something but then her eyes widened. "Oh! My *bruder* is here."

"Which one?" she teased, glancing around behind her.

Her heart sank. Well, of course it had to be Junior. Kaylene might have been one of eight kids, but there seemed to be only one of them that Miriam was destined to see. The very man who reminded her of everything she had always longed for.

When he caught her eye, he looked just as taken aback. "Hi, Miriam."

"Hello, Junior."

"You two look like you've been working hard."

"We surely have." Miriam smiled at Kaylene. "And we've been getting to know each other, too. I've enjoyed it *verra* much."

Junior met her eyes for a long moment, his own gaze warm and filled with gratitude. Then he crouched down so he was almost eye level with his sister. "How are you, Kay?"

"I'm *gut*."

"I'm glad about that."

"I didn't know you were going to come get me, though. I thought Micah was."

"Yeah, well, Micah got busy so I said I'd come." He turned to Miriam. "So, am I too early? I didn't mean to interrupt."

"You didn't. We were finished."

"Oh! Oh, well, that's *gut*." Looking uneasy for the first time, he said, "Would you mind if I went inside to speak with Mary Kate for a moment?"

Though she knew she shouldn't be surprised, Miriam felt a flash of disappointment. She'd never tell Kaylene, but she suspected that there was only one reason Junior had come to the schoolhouse instead of one of his brothers or sisters. "I don't mind."

"Why do you want to see her?" Kaylene asked with a little frown. "I haven't done anything wrong."

"I know that, Chipmunk. I wanted to talk to her about something else."

"What?"

He looked at Miriam in a silent plea for help.

She, however, wasn't about to get in the middle of this conversation. She smiled sweetly, content to watch him dig his way out.

After a moment, he said, "Mary Kate and I are becoming friends, that's why. And friends say hello to each other whenever they can."

"Oh." Kaylene nodded, but it was obvious to all three of them that no one believed his silly explanation.

Hoping to ease Kaylene's confusion, Miriam made a shooing motion with her hands. "If you're going to say hello to her, you had best go do that."

"*Danke.*" He smiled, then turned quickly toward the door of the schoolhouse.

Their book temporarily forgotten, Miriam watched him go inside with a frown. She didn't know what made her more uncomfortable, the fact that Junior liked her best friend and there was nothing she could do about it, or that here she was, still trying to do something nice for Junior when it was more than obvious he was never going to do anything like that for her.

"Miriam, you're frowning. Are you sad?" Kaylene asked.

Fearing there were now two bright splotches of color formed on her cheeks, she shook her head. "Not at all. I am just fine." She snuggled a little closer to Kaylene and pointed to the paragraph they'd been about to read. "Your turn, Chipmunk," she teased.

Kaylene giggled as she began to read again.

Chapter Fifteen ✧

Mary Kate glanced up from the novel she was reading when Junior entered the room. An expression of dismay flashed through her features before she smiled. "Hi, Junior."

"Hi." She looked so . . . so unexcited to see him, he hovered near the door. "I'm sorry. I thought you knew I was picking up Kaylene."

"I did. It's just that you're a little early. That's all."

"I thought, perhaps, we could talk a little bit before I took her home. Unless you're too busy, of course."

With a snap, she closed the book and shoved it into a drawer. "I'm not too busy to talk about Kaylene. Come on in."

As usual, he was struck by her beauty. Today she wore a purple dress. The dark color set off her green eyes and auburn highlights. Worried she might notice he was staring, he averted his eyes.

She moved to a long table with two rather small chairs next to it. "Please, sit down."

He sat. After she did, too, he said, "I visited with Kaylene and Miriam outside before I came in here. They seem to be getting along."

"I watched them out the window myself. Kaylene's been all smiles and giggles. But that's no surprise to me. Pretty much everyone is like that around Miriam."

Her reference made him think about just how easy it had been for him to open up to Miriam. And the revelations she'd shared about Mary Kate. He decided to tread carefully. "Mary Kate, I really did come in to . . . to talk with you. But not about my sister."

She stared at him blankly.

It wasn't often that he felt at a complete loss for words, but that's how he was feeling, and it seemed to be what happened when he was around Mary Kate. Perhaps this was what it was like to be in love? You wanted to impress the other person so much you hardly knew what to say? It was too bad he didn't enjoy it much.

He ached to ask her about her ex-boyfriend. Yearned to understand more about her, about what made her tick. But there was no way he would betray Miriam's confidence.

So, he cleared his throat. "So, Mary Kate. Um, what do you do when you're not working?"

"Nothing much. I don't know too many people yet."

"Maybe after church on Sunday we could go to Anderson's Apple Farm."

A line formed between her brows, marring her almost perfect face. "What is there?"

The answer was perfectly obvious. Apples. With his sisters, he would have teased them something awful. Even with Miriam, he would have joked about the question.

He tempered his response with Mary Kate, though. After all, she was new to Sugarcreek. "You can pick apples there."

Her eyes brightened, then it was firmly tamped down. "Oh. I don't really cook."

"Do you eat?" he teased.

"I'm not fond of apples, so I don't think it would be a *gut* idea."

"Oh." Finally, he decided to be straightforward. Now that he understood her reticence, he yearned for it to be out in the open. He felt sure that if she understood how he was used to looking out for others, how he was used to being leaned on, she would finally turn toward him.

"Mary Kate, have I offended you in some way I don't know about? It must be obvious that I've been trying to get to know you better."

She looked down at her folded hands before meeting his eyes. "Junior, I am sorry. I should have told you this some time ago. The truth is that I don't want to date anyone right now."

"Why is that?" He held his breath, waiting for her to finally tell him the truth.

"Well, I used to see someone in Millersburg. Things didn't end well between me and him."

"What happened?"

After a brief pause, she shook her head. "I'd rather not say. But please know that it's because

155

of him that I don't want to date anyone anytime soon. He, uh, left me feeling a bit wary when it comes to men."

"Have you ever considered that you don't need to be wary around all men?"

"Yes. But you need to realize that I'm not being coy. At the moment I just don't have it in me to even ponder a new relationship."

"Maybe, sometime soon, you should give someone else a try."

"Junior, have you listened to a single word I said?"

"Oh, *jah*. But I'm hoping you'll come around to my way of thinking soon."

"It might be a while."

"That's okay. See, I've got time."

For some reason, his confident statement didn't sit well with her. "Junior . . ."

"How about we have *kaffi* or *tay* one afternoon? That's pretty harmless."

"Junior—"

"Or pie. We could go to the Sugarcreek Inn and have a slice of pie? Miriam will probably be there." He held up a hand. "And we won't even think about anything other than possibly becoming friends. Surely you could use another friend, right?"

At last, she nodded. "I think you might have a point. I could use another friend."

"So, what do you say?"

"Okay, I will go with you to the Sugarcreek Inn."

Feeling like he'd just won a long race, he grinned. "Great. Next week, when I pick up Kaylene from her reading lesson, I'll come see when you want to go."

"That would be fine."

He smiled at her before he turned and walked out, feeling like he was ten feet tall.

He could hear her chuckling as he exited, and he wondered if she was laughing at his eagerness or if she felt happy and hopeful, too.

When he got back outside to the picnic table, his sister and Miriam were packing up Kaylene's things. "You're just in time," Miriam said with a happy smile. "We just finished the first chapter."

By her side, his little sister looked happier than he'd seen her in quite some time. "We're reading *Little Women*, Junior. And guess what?"

"What?"

She lowered her voice. "I'm starting to be able to read some of it pretty good."

"You can read a lot of it pretty good," Miriam corrected. "All you needed was a little bit of practice, that's all. I'm proud of you."

Kaylene looked back at Miriam with stars in her eyes.

"You'll come back next week and read with me again?"

"If you want me to, I will."

"I want you to," Kaylene said.

Miriam squeezed her hand. "Then we shall meet again next week."

"Thank you again, Miriam," he said. "You really are a life saver, in more ways than one."

"That's what friends are for, *jah*?" she asked right before she turned and gathered her tote bag.

When Kaylene went inside to say good-bye to Mary Kate, Junior noticed that Miriam had a thick bandage on her arm. Alarmed, he grasped it. "What happened?"

Miriam stiffened at his touch, then looked at her arm with something akin to disdain. "This? It's nothing. Just a burn."

A burn? Worry spread through him. "How did you get it?"

She chuckled. "In the kitchen, of course." Giving him a look that pretty much said he knew nothing, she murmured, "It's what happens when you cook for a living. One of the oven racks got me when I was pulling out a tray of biscuits."

"That sounds serious. And painful. Did you see the *doktah*?"

"Of course not." She gave him another strange look, then grinned. "Ah, now, here's our girl!"

"Teacher said she was proud of me, too, Junior," Kaylene said with a broad smile.

With effort, he forced his attention from

Miriam and to his little sister. "That makes three of us then," he said. "Ready to go home?"

"Uh-huh." She gave Miriam a little wave. "Bye!"

"Good-bye to you both. See you soon."

Junior gave a small wave before he picked up Kaylene's tote and they started walking. Almost immediately, Kay started chattering like a June bug.

He didn't say anything. Actually, he was kind of afraid to.

Because at the moment there was only one woman his mind kept returning to.

And it sure wasn't Mary Katherine Hershberger.

Chapter Sixteen ✟

A few mornings later, Claire walked out to the barn with a large mug filled with coffee in her hands. "Levi came home late again last night."

"*Gut matin* to you, too," Junior replied sarcastically, though he took the mug she offered with a grateful heart. After a fortifying sip, he said, "I'm guessing you want me to deal with him?"

"Yep."

"Any reason you don't want to?"

"Yep." Claire raised her eyebrows. "I'm, ah, fairly sure our Levi was with a girl last night."

"Who?" This was news to him. He hadn't heard that Levi had his eye on any particular girl.

"Between you and me, I don't think it was a special girl. Just an easy one."

He groaned. Like he wanted to have a conversation this morning about that. "Claire—"

"You're the oldest boy. Plus, you've already been through this with Randall, Micah, and Neil." She smiled sweetly, obviously imagining that her smile took the sting out of her words.

What was unsaid was that Randall had always had his eye on one girl, Elizabeth Nolt. Micah seemed to care only about mathematical theories, and Neil truly preferred to spend time with his animals than to spend time with girls. "Where is Levi?"

"Struggling to get dressed and come help you in the barn." She lowered her voice. "By the way, he's lookin' a bit green around the gills. I think he was drinking last night, too."

Junior sighed. "I don't think siblings should let other siblings have their *rumspringa*. This is the last thing I want to deal with right now."

Claire's voice gentled, though her words stayed sharp. "You know that we promised to stop complaining about our lot in life years ago."

"I hear you." He paused. "Save me a plate of breakfast, wouldja?"

"I already have." Her voice brightened as they watched their sixteen-year-old brother open the kitchen door and start a very slow walk toward the barn. "Ah, here he is. Good luck."

He grunted as he watched Levi pass Claire without a word, then attempt to pass him by in the same way. The moment Levi was within arm's length, Junior snaked a hand out and grabbed his shoulder. "Not so fast, little *bruder*."

"What?"

"We need to talk."

"Why?" His voice turned belligerent. "What did Claire come out here to tell you?"

"Only that you came in late last night."

Levi shrugged off his hand. "It weren't all that

late. Besides, I'm here now, aren't I? Ready to do more chores."

Junior bit back a dozen responses as he struggled for patience. At last he pointed to a rake. "Come with me, we've got to muck stalls."

As Claire mentioned, Levi looked a little green. "You haven't already done them?"

"Nope." Feeling more pleased about his brother's discomfort than he probably should, he murmured, "I waited for you."

Levi picked up the rake and entered the first empty stall. He wrinkled his nose. "It smells like—"

"Watch your mouth, Levi."

His brother pursed his lips and slowly began to rake the straw on the ground. Junior leaned over the rail and watched for a good five minutes. Then, just as Levi was scooping up a good amount of soiled straw into the wheelbarrow, he seized his chance. "Were you drinking last night?"

"*Jah.*"

"What?"

"Just a couple of beers. It weren't nothing."

"You shouldn't be drinking."

"Everyone has a beer or two when they're sixteen, Junior."

He hadn't. He'd been too busy trying to be a mother to all his younger siblings. He hadn't had time to do much but work, clean, cook, and try to be a whole lot wiser and smarter than he was.

But there was no way he was going to put that guilt on his brother. It wasn't Levi's fault that Junior had had to raise him.

So he held his tongue.

Levi stepped out of the stall, gave him a long, steady look of resentment, then marched into the next stall. "Must be nice, standing around and watching me do all the work."

"It's great. Fantastic."

"I bet."

"So, who were you with last night?"

"You know. My friends."

"Any girls?"

Levi leaned the rake next to the side of the stall. "What, exactly, did Claire tell you?"

"That she thought you were with a girl. I want to know who."

For the first time, Levi flushed with embarrassment. "She's no one you know."

"Is she English?"

Levi stared at him, obviously deciding whether or not to give him a straight answer. At last, he shrugged. "*Jah*. Her name is Kendra."

"Is she your girlfriend?"

"*Nee*."

"Then what is she to you?"

"She's just a girl, Junior." Levi shrugged. "She's nothing special. We just hung out together last night."

"If you hung out, she probably expects that you like her."

Levi sighed. "Junior, I'm not like you. I don't want to always be here working."

"I'm not always here working." Though, he kind of always was.

"You surely aren't courting." With a glare, he said, "Why not? Why don't you ever spend time with girls?"

"I have. But I've been kind of busy around here, you know."

"Well, it sure doesn't seem like you even care about girls."

"I've been spending time with Mary Kate Hershberger."

"That's one girl."

"I've been spending time with Miriam Zehr, too."

Levi stilled. "Do you like Miriam?"

"We're friends, nothing more," he said, matter-of-fact.

"Do you like Mary Kate more than Miriam?"

Sure Levi was being a little snide, Junior sucked in a breath, ready to champion Miriam and give Levi a talking-to about respecting women . . . when he realized that Levi wasn't being sarcastic at all. Rather, he was genuinely curious about Junior's thoughts on love and romance. "I don't know," he replied, then immediately felt even more awkward. "Um, I guess I find Mary Kate attractive and intriguing. And I think she needs me." And that was important because he liked being needed.

"You don't feel any of that with Miriam?"

"I think of her as a friend. I mean, as a good friend." Thinking about their conversation when he'd told her about Levi's nightmares, he added, "The thing with Miriam is that she is easy to talk to. And she's got a calm, practical way about her that always makes me think that everything is going to be okay."

Levi didn't look impressed. "But I thought those were things a man wanted to have in a relationship. You don't?"

"Of course I do."

"Is Mary Kate that way?"

"I'm not sure. I don't know her all that well." But he had a very good idea that *calm* and *practical* were not the best descriptors for her. Feeling a bit like he was the confused teenager, Junior added, "Mary Kate is really pretty."

Levi scoffed. "Miriam has a real pretty smile."

"You've noticed it?" When would he have noticed her smile?

Levi shrugged. "Well, sure. She smiles at us when we eat at the restaurant. And she smiled at me one morning at church when I couldn't sit still 'cause it was so hot and I was getting sweaty."

"She does have that way about her, doesn't she?" Junior murmured. "She's observant."

"I guess." Levi shrugged again. "I think it's mainly that Miriam is nice, you know? Everyone likes her."

"That is true." Annoyed that he sounded a bit surprised by this revelation, he said, "Kaylene has grown real fond of her. Miriam has been helping Kay with her reading."

"Kay told me." He rolled his eyes. "Kay talks about Miriam all the time now."

"I didn't realize that."

Levi gave him a look. "You're not the only one who looks out for her, you know." Before Junior could comment on that, Levi said, "Junior, you ought to let Miriam come over here to work with Kaylene."

"You think?"

"*Jah*. Then Kaylene doesn't have to sit in the school yard all afternoon. Kids will tease her, you know."

"You know what? That's a good idea. I'll talk to Miriam next time I see her."

"*Gut*." Levi picked up the rake again. "So, am I in trouble?"

"You will be if you don't settle down some. Stop drinking and remember to be respectful of the girls."

"Respectful?" He grinned.

To his embarrassment, Junior felt his neck heat. "You know what I'm talking about, Levi," he muttered. "Don't do anything stupid. Or anything that would have made our mother be ashamed of you."

He sighed. "I'll settle down, I promise—if you tell Claire not to be sticking her nose into my business. Tell her we already talked, wouldja?"

"I'll tell her to leave you alone. But if you mess up again? I'm going to make you muck stalls with her next time." After sharing a smile with his brother, he pushed away from the stall. "I'm going to go eat breakfast."

"Hey, I'm hungry, too. Do I have to finish this stall before I go in?"

"Yep."

"Because?"

"Because you're sixteen and I am not," he called out over his shoulder as he left the shadows of the barn and entered the morning sunshine.

Chapter Seventeen ✗

He was still thinking about Levi's idea of Miriam coming to the house to help Kaylene when he, Beverly, Claire, and Joe went to the Sugarcreek Inn for lunch.

They'd all been in town for various reasons. Beverly and Claire had needed to get some canning supplies at the Graber Country Store. Joe had come along because he'd wanted to spend some time with Beverly.

Junior was shopping on a Wednesday because he needed to pick up some medicines at the vet. And, well, he wanted to keep an eye on Joe and Beverly, too. He didn't mind that Joe and Beverly were now spending almost every moment they could together. Everyone in the family knew Joe's intentions were honorable, and Junior was even looking forward to the day when he could refer to Joe as his brother.

But that didn't mean he thought his sister and best friend didn't need a little supervision.

When they'd met at the restaurant, the other three had wasted no time in filling him in on some of the news around town. Some, like the fact that the bank was closing, was old news. Other news, like the rumor that Judith Knox had just suffered a miscarriage, was whispered in hushed voices. All of them vowed to stop by the store sometime in the next few days, just to see if there was any way they could help out the family.

After Marla came by and took their orders for soup and sandwiches, the conversation had led to a variety of other subjects—mainly discussed by Beverly and Joe. Though Claire seemed perfectly content to listen to their prattling, Junior's attention drifted. He might be happy that the two were falling in love, but he sure didn't intend to talk about their relationship while he ate!

Instead of listening to their chatter, Junior located Miriam. She was dressed today in a raspberry-colored dress and matching apron. A bandage still decorated her forearm, but it didn't seem to be bothering her.

Relieved about that, he watched her work. She was as busy as a bee, bringing out freshly baked pies for the bakery counter, greeting customers, and taking orders from two sets of tables at the back of the restaurant.

It looked to him like she was single-handedly doing about four jobs at the same time.

And then there was that moment when she stopped to chat with an elderly couple near the window. The couple was obviously a little hard of hearing, and to his amusement, Miriam had to repeat herself again and again every time she answered their questions.

But through it all, she never looked irritated. No, if anything, she looked, well, happy. And, to his surprise, kind of pretty. There had been that one instance when she was standing in the path of a beam of light shining from one of the sparkling windows. For a split second, it illuminated her smile. Highlighted how smooth her skin was. Her quiet blush.

And then she laughed and he couldn't look away.

In spite of his best efforts to remain detached, he found himself being just as charmed by her as the couple she was chatting with was.

He was still staring at her, thinking about what Levi had said about her, and about how a girl he'd known forever could suddenly be a person he couldn't seem to stop staring at, when Joe nudged him in the ribs. Hard.

He jerked. "What was that for?"

"I had to do something to get your attention."

"I was paying attention. Sort of."

Claire's lips curved upward. "Junior, are you ever going to join the conversation . . . or do you intend to only sit and stare at Miriam Zehr?"

That brought him up short. "I haven't been staring at her."

Beverly smirked. "Oh, yes you have."

"What's going on?" Joe asked. "You're going to her house, talking with her at church, and watching her work. I'm starting to think you don't just want her help catching Mary Kate's attention."

His collar was beginning to feel a little snug.

Irritated that he was the focus of their humor, he mentally rolled his eyes. Why had the four of them even decided to go out for lunch, anyway? It wasn't like he had much time for it. He had more than enough work to do on the farm. He should have just eaten a plate of leftovers instead of letting himself be talked into a meal of fresh soup.

"You sure seem pretty closemouthed. Cat got your tongue, *bruder*?" Claire teased.

Sipping his water, he was just about to firmly put their antics behind him when the three of them exchanged glances and chuckled again.

Then he lost his patience. "What, *exactly,* is so amusing?"

Joe and Beverly looked away. But Claire, being Claire, met his gaze head-on.

"You are." She held up a hand. "And don't be so touchy. I simply find it amusing that after all these years, you've suddenly become aware of someone who has been right under your nose all along."

Beverly's eyes twinkled with what could only be described as sisterly glee. "It's sweet."

"I don't do anything 'sweet.' "

"I'm not saying there's anything wrong with you suddenly developing an affection for

Miriam. I think it would be wonderful," Claire murmured, looking as full of herself as ever. "She's a wonderful person. She would also fit in very well with our family. I approve."

"And we all know she's always had a bit of a crush on you," Beverly added.

One sister teasing him was irritating. Two? It was making him annoyed. "*Nee*. No, she has not."

"I'm afraid she has, *bruder*. For pretty much all our lives, Miriam has had her eye on you. Heaven knows why." Two years older, Claire loved being right and always had. She also loved to tease him about everything and anything.

"You know how much she's done for Kaylene. Plus, she's helping me get to know Mary Kate. That's why we've been talking so much," he said.

"Too bad your visit with Mary Kate went so poorly after church," Joe snickered. "Either Miriam didn't describe you well to Mary Kate or Mary Kate wasn't as interested in you as you hoped."

"Mary Kate had to do a lot of schoolwork on Sunday. That's all."

His sisters exchanged looks again.

Beverly spoke, almost maintaining a straight face. "And you had to go over to Miriam's house again to get that information, didn't you?"

Now he felt himself flushing, too. "What's wrong with you guys? We're just friends."

Raising his chin a bit, he said, "Men and women can be friends without there being anything romantic, you know. It's not like we're teenagers. We are, after all, in our twenties."

Joe coughed. "You're right. And if it looked like that was all you had in common I wouldn't think a thing about your new friendship." He lowered his voice. "But I've seen the way you are looking at her today, Junior. You may have started a friendship with Miriam to get to Mary Kate, but there's something different in your eyes when you look at Miriam now."

"Miriam is a nice person," he pointed out.

"Yes, she is. Mighty nice." Joe folded his arms over his chest. "I never said she wasn't."

Tired of being their source of amusement, he continued, "She's smart, too. And a *gut* friend. Why, she's the type of person to bend over backward to help someone in need."

"She's the best," Beverly agreed.

"*Wunderbaar*!" Claire grinned.

Yes, Junior realized, Miriam Zehr was *wunderbaar*.

So much so, that it was kind of too bad that he was sure they were only meant to be friends.

Beverly must have sensed his dismay. She sighed. "We're only teasin' you, Junior. We don't mean any harm. Don't be so touchy."

Now thoroughly irritated, he glared at his sister.

He knew he should just keep his mouth shut but he didn't want to take a chance that this line of teasing would continue. "Miriam has been a good friend to me, even though she knows I never had any interest in her. I mean, it's not her fault that I like her friend a whole lot more than her. And even though she's not the prettiest girl in town, I'm sure she'll find someone suitable someday."

But even as he said the words, he flushed. That wasn't really what he'd told Levi. And it wasn't exactly what he'd been thinking either.

He sat up straighter when he noticed his sisters and Joe staring at him with matching horrified expressions.

Then wished he'd kept his big mouth shut when he saw why they were staring.

Miriam stood right behind him, holding a blasted basket of rolls—the rolls he'd once told her he liked so much.

It was painfully obvious that she'd heard every word he'd said.

Closing his eyes, Junior asked the Lord to give him a quick burst of strength. He hoped the Lord was of a mind to give him his wish quickly, too.

Because at the moment, he had no idea how he was ever going to make this situation better.

Chapter Eighteen ✏

Standing in the middle of the restaurant, a basket of rolls in her hands, Miriam wished she were absolutely anywhere else in the world.

And if that wasn't possible, she wished she could have at least wished the rest of the customers away.

Because at the moment, it felt as if pretty much everyone in Sugarcreek, Ohio, now knew exactly what Junior Beiler thought of her.

Her heart was pounding so hard she was sure it was going to pop out of her chest. Her hands were shaking. But from somewhere deep inside herself, she found a secret storage of strength. And used that to make herself look at Junior. And at his sisters. Then, finally, at Joe.

Junior scrambled to his feet. "Miriam, ignore what I just said, would ya? It, ah, didn't come out the right way. . . ."

"And what, do you think, would have been the right way?"

His cheeks flushed. "I mean, I didn't realize you were standing there. I mean . . . I mean I'm really sorry."

"We were teasing him about something," Claire said, her voice contrite. "We were teasing him and I'm afraid he spoke without thinking."

Miriam supposed that should make her feel better, but it didn't.

Now Joe stood up. "Miriam, please ignore all of us and try to forget it. I know I will."

Miriam spied Jana looking at their group curiously from over at the hostess table. It was time to smooth things over, and she knew instinctively that she was going to have to be the person to do it.

She didn't know why she was so upset and embarrassed anyway. She'd overheard Junior say she wasn't pretty. And that was true, she supposed. She would be the first person to admit she needed to eat less baked goods and put on her tennis shoes a bit more. But it still hurt.

"I, um, I came to give you these rolls," she blurted before handing them to Joe. Then she turned on her heel and strode back to the kitchen, taking care to keep her face an expressionless mask.

By the time she walked through the wide swinging doors, she'd drawn blood on her lip. She'd been biting her bottom lip as hard as she could in order to hold off the tears.

She was so irritated with herself.

Perhaps she should have known better by now. Here she was, a grown woman in her twenties, and she was still acting as dumb as a doorknob where Junior was concerned. After a couple of conversations, she'd assumed they were truly friends now.

But obviously only she thought of him that way.

A smarter woman would have learned by now to keep her distance from him.

The simple truth was that if he hadn't taken a shine to her by now, he surely wasn't ever going to. Junior Beiler was never going to like her in the way she'd fantasized about.

Luckily, the other women in the kitchen were working hard so they didn't see how distressed she was. Happy to keep to herself, she pulled the canisters of flour and sugar closer and set to make sugar cookies. As she beat in the eggs and vanilla, then finally the flour mixture, her mind focused on her new goal: she needed a change. She needed something to look forward to, something to be excited about. Something new.

Because it was painfully apparent that her current situation was never going to change. At least, not anytime soon.

Looking up from the batch of bread she was kneading, Ruth frowned. "Miriam, I think you look a bit pale. Do you think you're getting sick?"

"I'm not sure."

"If you're not sure, you probably are. You know what? Maybe you should go home and take a break. Everyone needs a break now and then."

In the five years that she'd worked at the Inn,

Miriam had never once gone home sick. It wasn't in her nature to shirk her responsibilities. It wasn't in her nature to run. But maybe she did need a break.

If she stayed, she was going to have to face Junior again. Maybe have to talk to his sisters and pretend that nothing was wrong at all. If she left, she wouldn't.

Suddenly, it was the easiest decision she'd made in weeks. She grabbed her cloak, slipped it over her shoulders, then hastily wrote Jana a note. After placing it neatly in the middle of Jana's desk, she darted out the back door.

And instantly felt relief.

Feeling like Junior's words were biting her heels, she walked briskly through the maze of parked cars on the lot. Past the pair of buggies hitched near the field, the two horses nickering a bit as she walked by.

As she picked up her pace, felt the muscles in her thighs burn a bit from the unaccustomed exercise, Miriam made a new vow. At last, she was going to stop mooning over Junior. She was going to stop fancying herself in love with him. Some way or somehow. Yes. She was going to do that, if it was the very last thing she ever did.

The next day, right after he finished his chores, Junior told Micah that he had an important errand to run. Then, with a new resolve, he walked to

Miriam's. He was dreading the visit, but not as much as he dreaded another hour feeling guilty. All night long he'd tossed and turned. Both the things he'd said at the restaurant and Miriam's reaction to them reverberated in his head. No matter how many ways he tried to excuse his slip of the tongue, he knew there was no excuse. He owed Miriam an apology.

As the sun continued its rise over the horizon, signaling the start to another day, he practiced his apology. He hoped she would find it in her heart to forgive him, though he wasn't sure if he deserved her forgiveness or not. His words had been unkind—and had been said out loud in her place of work.

Yes, it had been an especially bad moment.

When he approached the house he spied her immediately.

She was holding a watering can and looked to be watering a set of hanging baskets filled with bright pink and purple petunias. Every time she stretched on her tiptoes, she wore a look of irritation, like she wished she were two inches taller.

Or maybe she was simply irritated about his visit.

As he watched her, Junior couldn't help but compare it to the expression she'd worn on his first visit. Then, her eyes had glowed with happiness and she'd smiled softly at him.

Now it was obvious that she'd wished he would turn around and go.

Had he actually hoped she'd easily forgive him with a smile, and let him go on his way, his conscience alleviated?

To his shame, yes, he had.

Before she had the chance to send him on his way, he started his speech. "Miriam, we need to talk."

She set her watering can down. "I'm not so sure about that."

"Listen, yesterday, my sisters kept teasing me," he said quickly. "And though I know better, they started getting the best of me. Some of the things I said didn't come out the way I had meant for them to. I wasn't thinking."

She folded her arms across her chest. "Junior, let's be honest. It hardly matters what you think about me. I mean, it's not like we've ever been anything to each other."

"No, we've been friends—"

She cut him off. "Junior, we've never been *gut* friends. Not really. You and I both know that."

"But we could be good friends now." Thinking about how he felt about her, about how far they'd already come, he added, "I mean, I think we are friends now."

She closed her eyes for a brief moment, just as if she was trying to gather her patience. "You know what? You came over, and I appreciate that. But I think it's time we said good-bye. I've got a lot of other things to do besides chat with you." And with that, she turned on her heel and reached for the door handle.

Without thinking, he stepped forward and grabbed her hand. Wrapped his palm around hers. "Wait a minute, wouldja?"

She stared down at their linked hands like he'd just given her a bad case of poison ivy. With one fierce tug, she freed her hand.

Of course he let her go. But he still wasn't ready to say good-bye just yet. "Can't we sit for a moment and talk? Please?"

For a second, she looked tempted. Her eyes turned languid, almost warm.

He, in turn, felt that new, almost familiar pull toward her that now seemed to be a part of his life. Hope filled him. Reminding him that every-thing could work out.

Then she shook her head. "We've already talked. You've apologized. I have accepted your apology. You can now go back to your sisters or to your friends or whoever and feel good about yourself."

"That's pretty harsh."

Her voice turned strained. "Junior, I'm simply trying to say that you don't owe me anything. Can't we leave it at that?"

"*Nee*. Miriam, I didn't mean to make it sound

like I didn't think you were pretty. I certainly didn't mean it."

"Can this not be about you?"

Ouch. "Listen, all I'm trying to say is that I made a mistake, I feel badly about it, and I want us to get back to how we were."

"Junior—"

"Please? I know I'm an idiot. But I'm not all bad. All I know is that I don't want there to be any tension between us."

Miriam sighed. Watched him squirm under her gaze.

"Junior, how about this? How about we simply forget that conversation ever happened? I think that would be easiest for both of us."

"Do you think that's possible?"

"Of course it is possible," she said. "Actually, I doubt I'll ever think about it again. Now, I really do have to go. Good-bye, Junior. And good day."

As he stood there, trying to discern what she really meant, she opened the door and walked inside her house. All without a backward glance his way.

The rejection hurt. Feeling like he'd just run a marathon only to trip two feet from the finish line, he slowly walked back home.

Today was the first time Miriam Zehr hadn't looked at him with stars in her eyes. It was the first time he hadn't been able to smile at her and get one in return.

Instead, she'd treated him as if he wasn't anyone special to her.

His footsteps slowed as he realized he'd just lost something really important. But the worst of it was that for most of his life, he hadn't even realized what he'd had.

Chapter Nineteen ✓

"Good-bye, Scholars," Mary Kate said as she stood at the door to the schoolhouse watching her students file out the door promptly at three o'clock. "We had a *gut* day today. Get some sleep and I'll see you bright and early tomorrow morning."

"Bye, Teacher," little Emma said, followed by another two girls. "See you tomorrow."

"Indeed," she said with a smile. "See you then."

When the very last of her students left and she was completely alone, she sagged in the privacy of the doorway.

At last. Another day was over.

Some days, it seemed like it took everything she had to make it through to three o'clock with a smile on her face.

Though she wished it wasn't so, Mary Kate knew she wasn't a very good teacher. She didn't have the knack to organize twenty students at once. She became easily frustrated, too.

And then there was the added knowledge that she never seemed able to completely relax. Some evenings, she felt so stiff and sore, only the hottest and lengthiest of showers helped ease her stiff muscles.

But of course, much of her stress had nothing to

do with her job. Instead, it had everything to do with Will. No matter how hard she tried to think of other things, he always lingered in the back of her mind. She worried about him discovering her. Worried that he would still be lurking in the periphery of her existence for years to come. Worried that she would never be entirely free of him.

Just as she got herself worked up again, her favorite verse from the Psalms drifted into her mind.

The righteous person faces many troubles, but the Lord comes to the rescue each time.

The words were true and settled her like little else did. Yes, that was what she needed to remember. To pray about. If only she could remind herself that the Lord would always come to her rescue, no matter how difficult the situation, she could finally breathe easier.

Perhaps she could be herself once again. At last.

"There's nothing you can do, Mary Kate," she reminded herself. "All you can do is grade some papers and plan for tomorrow. And hope that one day soon you will be proud of yourself."

She'd just turned away from the doorway when a shadow appeared to her right. Anxious, she scanned the area. Gazed out beyond the wide sloping hill, searched the dense woods just beyond.

But she didn't see anything. Only felt the vague sense of unease.

"Hello?" she called out. As her voice echoed through the emptiness, she felt a bit silly. After all, if someone was out there who did not want to be seen, would they truly answer back?

The seconds seemed to pass like minutes as she waited in vain. The hair on the back of her neck prickled. Her unease was turning into full-fledged fright.

"You have got to get a hold of yourself, Mary Kate," she cautioned herself yet again. "You are letting your imagination run away with you." Almost believing her words, she turned around. Determined to get her work done and then head home.

A twig snapped.

She froze as goose bumps appeared on her arms. Was that her imagination? Her fear talking?

Or had Will found her?

She was tempted to call out his name, tempted to call out anything. But she feared if she did give voice to her greatest fear it would make it all seem a lot more real.

Instead, she stood frozen. Half waiting, half watching for the last person on earth she wanted to see step out of the shadows.

Then she heard the unmistakable sound of footsteps on gravel on the side of the yard. Whoever had been there was walking away.

It took everything she had to dart inside and run to the bank of windows. Part of her didn't want to see the evidence. It would be so much easier to call herself a silly fool and pretend that nothing was wrong.

But she'd done that before and had learned that it came with a heavy price.

Stepping closer, she peered out the windows. At first she saw nothing, and she breathed easier.

But then she saw a footprint in the damp ground next to the building. Someone had been there. And he had intentionally not answered her. He'd wanted her to be scared, to feel helpless. To wonder what was going to happen next.

Which gave her all the information she needed. Will Lott had come to Sugarcreek, and sooner or later, he would make sure he didn't leave alone.

I'm so glad you and Ben decided to come over for a spell, Judith," her mother said as they finished hemming a new dress for Clara, cousin Tim's wife. "I miss spending time with you."

"I am glad we came too," Judith replied. "Ben and I have enjoyed being here. You know how much Ben loves being around the family."

Her mother chuckled. "I hope he will say the same when you two go back home. Maggie is at his side at every meal, and Anson has been constantly on his heels, asking question after question."

Judith grinned, liking the way her mother described her brother's determined shadowing. She loved seeing Ben interact with the kids. "Ben adores little Maggie. She can do no wrong in his eyes. As for Anson? Don't tell anyone, but I think Ben kind of likes Anson's hero worship."

"Truly?"

"Truly. Ben's never had a brother, of course, and Anson is easy to be with."

"He sure is patient with him. Only Ben would allow Anson to help him stack wood."

"No, only Ben could convince Anson to spend three hours cutting wood, bringing it home, and stacking it." Judith shook her head. "I don't know how many times Josh and Caleb have tried to get Anson to do more work around the farm."

"Ben certainly has a way with that boy." Her mother's gaze turned softer. "Did you know Ben helped Maggie bake cookies yesterday?"

"I did. Because of his difficult family situation growing up, I think Ben sometimes feels he's not good enough. But little Maggie always reminds him that he's special to her. He's told me before that Maggie makes him feel like he's the brightest and tallest person in the room. She's really good for him."

Her siblings had been good for her, too, Judith reflected. At home, there was always commotion and hungry mouths to feed and arguments and laughter. And projects! "Sewing this dress for Clara has done me a world of good."

She held up the dress and pictured how pretty Clara would look in it. The fabric was a lighter shade of blue, almost a periwinkle. It looked fresh and bright—a perfect foil for the upcoming dreary months of winter.

"Hopefully it will brighten Clara's day, too. The good Lord knows she needs a little ray of sunshine."

Clara and Tim's twin girls were just getting over a terrible case of the chicken pox. For almost two weeks Clara had made oatmeal baths, cuddled crying and itchy children, read an insurmountable number of picture books, and heated jars and jars of soup that they'd canned last summer.

Now the girls were happy and almost healed. Just about back to normal. But Clara? She was exhausted.

Now, her mother, Josh's wife, Gretta, and Caleb's new bride, Rebecca, had decided to take Clara out for a girls' getaway the following weekend. They'd gotten a deal on one of the tourist cabins out in Charm and were going to take Clara there for a good dose of shopping and eating. Judith had been invited, too, but she'd declined the invitation. She wasn't quite ready to be away from Ben for an extended period of time.

To no one's surprise, Clara's husband, Tim, had thought this was a wonderful idea for his sweet wife. Once the travel arrangements had been made, Judith had mentioned that Clara would probably like a new dress for her day and evening out, too. Clara never did anything for herself.

In just an hour, Tim was going to stop by with Clara for supper, as were Caleb and Rebecca. They'd have a simple supper of meat loaf, mashed potatoes, and corn, followed by a chocolate cream pie. Then they were going to spring the trip on Clara.

Judith couldn't wait to see surprise light Clara's eyes—and happiness fill Tim's gaze as he watched her. It was such a pleasure to concentrate on other people for a change. She was so tired of being depressed and concentrating on her heartache. Though she understood that a period of mourning was only natural, she also realized that it was time to move forward. The Lord had a plan for each of them and it would be wrong of her to dwell on her disappointments for too long.

As her *mamm* touched the just finished hem of Clara's new dress, she said, "Clara is going to love this. Are you sure you don't want to change your mind about going with us to the cabin? Going on a girls' weekend might be good medicine for you, too."

"I'm sure. Being here has been enough of a vacation for me." Plus, her emotions were so topsy-turvy, she wasn't eager to be far from Ben. She knew she needed his hugs as often as possible.

"I'm so proud of you, Judith," her mother said, obviously choosing her words carefully. "I know your recovery hasn't been easy, but you do seem to have a bit of your spark back."

"I think it's coming back, too. It hasn't been easy, but it's getting better." She was done dwelling on her disappointment, at least with her family and friends. She was sure no one wanted to hear any more stories about how sad she was day after day. Everyone else had moved on. The only thing she'd gain by wallowing in her grief was more hours to sit alone by herself.

"I'm not sure why the Lord has decided that Ben and I can't have a baby, but I do feel certain that Got will lead me and show me His will."

"Those are wise words. And true," her mother murmured as Ben came into the kitchen, followed by Anson.

While Ben walked to her side and gently squeezed her shoulder, offering his quiet support, Anson breezed by without a word.

Their mother frowned. "Anson, say hello to your sister."

He skidded to a stop. "Hi, Judith."

"Anson." Sharing a smile with her mother, she

said, "What have you and Ben been doing all afternoon?"

"Manly things."

"Oh?" She peeked up at Ben, wondering what "manly things" entailed.

He rolled his eyes and clamped a hand on Anson's shoulder. "Nothing too important. We took a long walk and checked on the creek."

Anson nodded. "I told Ben all about how Ty and me almost drowned there a couple of years ago."

That awful day would always remain vivid in her memory. Sharing a look with her mother, she murmured, "That was quite an afternoon, indeed."

"Anyway," Anson said airily, "I'm getting something to eat now. I'm starving."

"Starving, hmm?" She couldn't help but grin. Her brother had been born hungry and very little got in between him and his food. Now that he was on the cusp of his teenage years, he seemed to be storing as much food as possible in his body for later use.

"Anson, we'll be eating in just an hour," their mother cautioned. "And I know you had something to eat just a few hours ago."

"Mamm, that was two hours ago."

Judith, to her surprise, found herself grinning. Anson said "two hours" the way some people said two years.

But her mother, at least, didn't seem too understanding. "I don't want you to spoil your supper."

He gave her a look that silently conveyed she was sillier than ever. "I'll still be hungry then, Mamm."

"Anson—"

"He'll eat, Mamm," Ben said with a wink. "He always does."

Her mother's cheeks pinkened the way they always did whenever her son-in-law called her "Mamm." Judith knew Ben's use of that name hadn't come easy . . . and it was also said with complete sincerity.

"Do you really think so?" her mother pressed. "Neither Caleb nor Joshua ever ate like Anson."

"I'm more than sure," Ben agreed. "This boy of yours is always hungry. I only brought him in here so he wouldn't start eating the hay in the barn."

Judith smiled at her husband as Anson filled up a large glass with milk and drank it in two gulps, grabbed a couple of apples, and one of the rolls on the countertop. Next he pocketed several peanut butter cookies.

Then, without another word, he gathered up his bounty and strode out the back door, the screen door creaking shut after him.

Her *mamm* rested her head against the back of her chair. "That boy is going to be the death of me."

"Don't be too hard on him. There's nothing wrong with enjoying *gut* food," Ben quipped. "You're *wonderful-gut* cook, Mamm."

"*Danke*, Ben."

After snatching a cookie, he winked at Judith again before he, too, went back outside.

"Just look at this," her mother exclaimed, motioning to the almost-empty jar of cookies, the one apple in the bowl, and the container of rolls that had been left unwrapped. "Those boys are going to eat me out of house and home."

"At least, after Anson, we only have Toby's teenage years to get through," Judith joked.

"If I ever survive Anson, I have a feeling I'm going to be too tired to cook," her mother said with a laugh. "You might have to do all the cooking for him."

"I'll be happy to, Mamm. So far, Toby is the easiest of us all."

"I do believe you are right, dear. I had best give praise for that, and often. He is my last boy and so far the easiest to raise."

Judith smiled weakly. Despite the brave face she put on, all this talk had reminded her that she would never have hungry boys of her own running through her kitchen. And that fact still broke her heart.

Chapter Twenty ✗

"Junior, why did you come all the way up to school to get me?" Kaylene asked as he walked her back from another tutoring session with Miriam. "I thought you were going to be working in the barn today."

"Well, it turns out that Micah and Randall have everything under control. Plus, you know how much I like to walk with you."

"What happened to Levi?" She wrinkled her nose. "He told me at breakfast that he was going to come get me."

He grinned. "He couldn't make it here, either."

"Is he in trouble?"

"Not at all." He touched her nose with one finger. "And do try not to sound so hopeful." She had a love-hate relationship with Levi. He was the closest to her age, which meant he was far less the father figure that Junior was and more of a pesky brother who liked to ignore her. "Neil recruited Levi's help with the lambs."

"And he listened?"

"*Jah*. For once," he replied with a chuckle. Ever since Levi had graduated from eighth grade and had started his *rumspringa*, he'd become a handful. With the exception of staying out too late and drinking the other night, he was doing nothing that the majority of the other boys and girls his age weren't also doing.

But it always amused Junior to hear Kaylene's perspective on Levi's behavior. Sometimes it seemed as if she had the least amount of patience with Levi.

"I'm not going to act like Levi when I'm his age," she said with a little shake of her head.

"I hope you don't. I'm going to be eight years older by then and too tired and old to give you lectures."

"Oh, Junior. You won't be that old."

"I suppose you're right. But I'm still going to hope that you'll be a good girl when you are sixteen."

"I will. I know it."

Grinning, he rested a comforting hand on her shoulder as they walked side by side on the narrow lane leading up to their farm. He'd meant to take the buggy to pick her up, but things had been pretty chaotic at the house when he'd left.

Besides, sometimes these walks were the best part of their days. In a full household like theirs, opportunities for private conversation were few and far between.

"Are things going any better with Claire?" he asked. Lately Claire had been after Kaylene to make her bed every morning, which, for some reason, was something their little sister didn't like to do.

"I get along with her fine." His little sister skipped ahead of him, then turned to walk backward. "Did you know that Randall is courting Elizabeth Nolt?"

"I know he took her out once or twice."

"He's taken her out more than that."

"Huh." He glanced at her curiously. It never failed to surprise him how the youngest member of their family always knew the most gossip. "Are they finally getting serious?"

"Maybe." After a pause, she got on her tiptoes. "I saw them kissing after church."

"Really?" Junior was torn between grinning and acting appropriately shocked by such behavior. "Did he see you?"

"Nope."

"You got lucky there."

"Yep. He would've gotten mad."

"He would've," Junior agreed. Half thinking to himself, he murmured, "I wonder who will be the first of us to get married. I had always assumed it would be Beverly, but now I'm not so sure. Maybe it will be Randall."

"I think it's gonna be Randall. Or maybe Beverly and Joe. She likes him a lot, you know."

"That is something I actually do know," he teased. "My vote is Beverly. And definitely not Claire. She's not seeing anyone, is she?"

"Nope. Claire is too picky. Well, she likes a

boy over in Charm, but they hardly ever see each other."

Kaylene was a font of information. "Who is that? Jay?"

"Uh-huh."

Before they knew it, they were good-naturedly analyzing everyone's love life, and Junior was getting an earful. As usual, Kaylene knew far more than he did.

He was amused to also realize that neither of them thought anything was strange about this. Kaylene was observant, and her manner and young age enabled her to fade into the background in a way the others never had.

"Junior, who are you going to marry?" she asked.

"I don't know." When he'd picked up Kaylene, he'd made a date with Mary Kate to go to the Sugarcreek Inn later on in the week. But ironically, he wasn't all that excited about it.

"Do you like Miss Mary Kate?"

"Well, I think she's real pretty. And I think I like her, but I'm not real sure that she's the girl for me. She's, um, fairly difficult to get to know." As he heard his words he felt a mild sensation of panic. He'd known that was how he was feeling, but to hear his thoughts said out loud surprised him.

Glancing down at his sister, he said, "Kay, do you like her?"

"Sort of." She shrugged, worrying him. Usually Kaylene liked everyone.

"That doesn't sound too good."

She tilted her little chin up, her light brown eyes, so like their father's, searching his face for a hint of what he wanted her to say. He stopped and knelt in front of her on the gravel path. "You can tell me anything, Kay. I promise."

She took a deep breath, then blurted, "I like her, but I don't like her being my teacher," she said at last. Her brow wrinkled. "Does that make sense?"

He thought back to his years in the very same school building where she now spent her days. All he could remember was being compared to Claire, Beverly, and Randall—and having to constantly watch out for the younger boys.

But try as he might, he couldn't remember thinking too much about his teacher, other than the fact that he'd wished Miss Hannah wouldn't rap his knuckles with a ruler or assign so much homework.

"I want to understand, Kaylene. But I don't."

Her expression shuttered. "Never mind."

"No, I want to hear what you have to say."

"You're gonna get *bays*, because everyone knows that you like her."

"I won't get mad. Like I said, I thought I liked her, but I'm not positive she's the right woman for me. So be honest—just like you usually are."

But instead of chuckling with him she looked even more wary. "I'm afraid you're going to say it's my fault."

"Kaylene, I won't. Now what is wrong?"

"She doesn't listen to me. She just gives me my assignment, and when I tell her I can't do it too good, she tells me to try it again."

Lowering her voice, she added, "But that's the problem, Junior. I don't know how to do it in the first place. And then when I ask someone else for help, she gets mad at me."

"Surely not." He was shocked. And it was becoming pretty evident that it didn't matter who he liked—he had a protective streak for his little sister about a mile long.

"She does," Kaylene whispered softly. "Today I couldn't go eat lunch with all the other *kinner*. I had to sit by myself because she said I had already done my talking for the day." She lowered her voice. "But I was only asking people what the directions were, 'cause I couldn't read them."

"Oh, Kay."

Eyes wide, she stared up at him, her expression sad and embarrassed . . . and full of hope, too. She needed him to believe in her, he realized.

"I'm real sorry, Junior," she mumbled.

A sick knot formed in his stomach, both at Kaylene's story and the fact that he was the one she was having to talk to instead of either of their parents. Once again, he wished he'd understood why the Lord had decided to take their parents at such young ages.

He had no idea how to handle problems with a teacher, or how to encourage a little girl without making her feel worse.

Pale, faint visions of his mother always helping him flashed through his mind, reminding him of how capable she was . . . and how far his efforts were from hers.

Little Kaylene needed someone like that in her life.

As the seconds passed and he kept his silence, weighing various ways to comment on what his sister said, he could feel her slowly losing faith in him.

When she dipped her chin onto her chest, visibly retreating into herself, Junior knew that he had to try. To do or say nothing more would be a terrible mistake.

"How are things going with Miriam?"

"*Gut*. I wish you wanted to marry her."

"What?" When her eyes widened, he rolled his shoulders and tried to sound more relaxed. "Um, why would you say something like that?"

Kaylene gave him a look that said he was a fool. "Junior, everyone likes Miriam! She's the best cook in the whole town and she's mighty nice."

"She sure is." It seemed everyone he talked to only had good things to say about Miriam Zehr. Kaylene, Joe, Levi, his sisters. Only now that she wanted nothing to do with him was he understanding that her kindness was something that he truly valued.

"I was over at the Kempfs' *haus* and Mr. and Mrs. Kempf are real nice to each other. So being nice is important when you get married, right?"

Her innocent comment broke his heart. Kaylene knew about families but not much at all about marriage. She was having to rely on her friends' parents for her education. "That's right," he murmured. "Kindness is important in any relationship, but most especially in a marriage."

"Plus, when she helps me read, she goes real slowly and listens. She's the best reading teacher I've ever had."

Her statement reminded him of the promise he'd made Levi. "You know what? What if we asked Miriam if she wouldn't mind coming to the farm to help you read? Then you wouldn't always have to stay after school for your lessons."

Kaylene's eyes widened. "You'd do that?"

"Of course I would, I'm your *bruder*."

"Junior, even though I'm not supposed to have favorites, you're my favorite *bruder*."

"I'm glad." He looked down at her, remembering when she was a tiny thing and he'd often carry her around the farm on his shoulders. "You're my favorite sister. But don't tell anyone that we have favorites. They might get *bedrohwa*, you know."

Solemnly she shook her head. "I won't tell anyone."

Two hours later, when he and Kaylene were sitting with the rest of the family at dinner, he shared another smile with her. To say his family was loud and gregarious was an understatement. Three or four different conversations continually happened at the same time, each one punctuated with laughter or general teasing.

Years ago his father had asked Robert Miller to build them a custom dining room table, big enough to hold all ten of them comfortably, and twelve to fourteen in a pinch.

He remembered the first time they'd all sat at the large oak table, with the twin benches on either side and the handsomely carved chairs gracing each end. He'd been fifteen and Levi had been just a baby. Kaylene hadn't even been thought of back then.

But as he'd sat next to his father, with Beverly on his right and ten-year-old Micah across from him, he remembered thinking that probably no one else had a family like his. He'd been glad about that.

Now that they were all full grown except for Kaylene, he felt even more assured about how they had all turned out. No, they weren't perfect. They were far from that!

But there was a life and an energy in his house

that he'd never witnessed anywhere else. And though he wished their parents were there with them, Junior realized that he and his siblings had carried on fairly well, all things considered.

Actually, he felt sorry for anyone who had to live by him- or herself.

It was okay that some of their personalities meshed and some clashed. It was okay that sometimes they disagreed and lost their patience with each other.

And it was okay that sometimes he felt as if he was the one who felt the burden of raising their little sister. Long ago, he had stopped wishing for things to be different.

Wishes and doubts and regrets had no place in a family such as theirs, and especially not for a man as blessed as he.

More than ever, he was thankful for his faith. For some reason known only to the Lord, He had decided to take their parents at a young age.

He'd also like to imagine that that was why the good Lord had given them so many family members. They complemented each other in the best of ways. And Junior certainly never felt alone.

Everyone else should be so lucky, he mused. Everyone else should be so blessed.

But just as he was giving thanks for being able to find peace with his family situation, he realized that he really was ready to build his own family. Some of it was because Mary Kate had arrived in town and caught his fancy. For so long, he'd been waiting for love to hit him like a bolt of lightning. Striking him with the surety that he'd found the perfect woman.

But now, he was starting to wonder if he'd wasted a lot of time simply overlooking what had been right in front of him all the while.

As the rest of his siblings continued to talk, Junior let his thoughts turn back to the conversation he'd had with Kaylene. Thought about how he'd asked Mary Kate out to eat and that even though she'd accepted, how, ironically, he hadn't felt all that excited about it.

He thought about Kaylene's statement about husbands and wives needing to be kind to each other.

And he knew Miriam would be very kind to whoever she ended up marrying.

"You okay down there, Junior?" Randall teased. "You've been awfully quiet."

Junior shook off his wayward thoughts with a grin. "You all have been talking so much I figured I'd just listen for a spell."

They all looked at him strangely but went back to debating Neil's goat's chances of placing in an upcoming stock show.

And within minutes he was back to thinking about two very different women and how they'd fit in at this very important table.

Chapter Twenty-one ♪

As usual, Miriam worked half a day on Saturday. Though she usually resented spending most of her Saturday at the restaurant, this time she was glad for the distraction. She needed to spend as much time as possible baking pies and serving meals to customers. Anything besides her current bad habit, thinking about Junior Beiler.

Further confusing things was her growing attachment to his little sister. She truly enjoyed helping Kaylene learn to read. Of course, any opportunity to reread *Little Women* felt like a gift. When she was Kaylene's age, she'd spent many an evening being swept away with the antics of Jo, Amy, Meg, and Beth.

Miriam had been curious to see how Kaylene felt about the story since she was from such a large family. Since she'd been practically raised as an only child, Miriam had been fascinated with the idea of having three sisters. She'd been envious of the characters' late-night chats and sharing of secrets.

But to Miriam's surprise, Kaylene had seemed unfamiliar with such things. It seemed she was a lot like Miriam—used to keeping her own company.

Also surprising was Mary Kate's lack of

interest in the lessons. Miriam had imagined that Mary Kate would have been supervising, or maybe even taking notes while Kaylene read. But instead, she stayed in the classroom.

She was still thinking about her friend's behavior when Mary Kate walked into the restaurant.

Miriam greeted her at the hostess desk. "Hi! I didn't know you had plans to come visit today."

"I hadn't planned on it, but I need to talk to you for a couple of minutes."

"I'm fairly busy right now. Is something wrong?"

"It's about Junior Beiler."

Her heart sank. Of course. The one person she didn't want to talk about. "What about him?"

"Well, I finally told him I'd go to supper with him."

"Here?"

"*Jah*." Mary Kate looked vaguely uncomfortable. "I told him I'd feel more comfortable here. Since you might be here, too."

Miriam struggled to keep looking pleasantly surprised. After all, Mary Kate had come here needing support. What kind of friend would she be if she didn't give that to her? "Well, if I'm working, I'll definitely keep a close eye on you both."

But of course, with all her heart, she hoped she would be off whatever night they came in.

Trying to still be a supportive friend, she prodded Mary Kate for more information. "What made you change your mind?"

Mary Kate sighed, looking worn down. "I think it might be a good experience. All I've been doing since I moved here is worrying about Will finding me and planning where to go next. But that's no way to live."

Feeling a bit petty because she'd only been worrying about herself, Miriam nodded. "You're right about that, Mary Kate."

"Besides, my mother wrote that she told Will where I was a few weeks ago. If he was that anxious to find me, he would've come to Sugarcreek by now. So, um, I'm starting to think I've been overreacting a bit."

"I see."

Mary Kate nodded. "So, I'm going to have supper with Junior. But while we're eating, I'm going to make sure he knows that I am glad for his friendship. But that is all I want."

Forgetting that she was supposed to be working, Miriam leaned closer to her friend. "Why would you tell him that?"

"You know why. I don't want to date anyone."

Happiness warred with guilt in her heart. "Well, I suppose you'll just have to take things one step at a time."

The corners of Mary Katherine's eyes crinkled. "I think you are right. Besides, we both know who should be courted by Junior Beiler. You two are perfect for each other."

Miriam was just about to protest, debating whether to tell her friend about Junior's harsh words in the restaurant, when Mrs. Kent walked over. "Miriam, are you on break right now and I didn't realize it?"

"Uh, *nee*. Sorry. I'll get back to work." Picking up her coffeepot, she gave Mary Kate a little wave good-bye. "Thanks for telling me what's going on."

"Anytime," Mary Kate said with a genuine smile before she walked out the front door.

After getting a fresh pot of *kaffi*, she started refilling customers' coffee cups. All the while thinking that coming to work had not given her the respite from her problems that she'd been seeking.

In a town this small, it seemed you could never get away from your life.

Miriam brought a thick blanket and a thermos of hot chocolate for her reading lesson with Kaylene. This was now their fifth lesson and she'd been enjoying her time with the eight-year-old so much.

Once she'd discovered that Kaylene was usually hungry and ready for an afternoon snack, Miriam had taken to bringing either a treat from the restaurant or preparing something from home. Today she had oatmeal scotchies.

Her mother had boxed up the cookies for her that morning, making Miriam feel more than a little guilty. She still hadn't found a way to tell her parents that she and Junior Beiler weren't really courting.

For the time being, Miriam was determined to enjoy each moment that she had with Kaylene. She was growing to really care about the little girl. She truly enjoyed spending time with her, and she enjoyed watching Kaylene learn to love reading, too.

Today they'd read about Beth getting scarlet fever. Kaylene's eyes had gotten as big as saucers as they'd read the part about the girls surrounding their sister and worrying about whether to send for their mother or not.

"Do you think there really is such a thing as scarlet fever, Miriam?" Kaylene asked quietly.

"Oh, *jah*. Not too many people get it anymore, though. And if they do, they go straight to the *doktah* for medicine."

"I hope I don't get it."

"I hope so, too. But since we don't have much scarlet fever going around Sugarcreek, I think you're safe enough."

"My mamm and daed died, you know."

"I know. And I'm sorry about that." Miriam reached over and squeezed the little girl's hand.

"Neither of them had scarlet fever. But they still died."

"We never know what God plans for us, do we?"

Kaylene shrugged. "Junior says our parents went to heaven early because they knew they had eight children to look after each other."

"You have a wonderful family, that's true. A lot of people would love to have so many brothers and sisters."

"Sometimes I wish I had a sister closer to my age, though."

"We all want things we don't have, Kay." Hoping to lighten the mood, Miriam fingered one of her dark curls that had sprung out of her *kapp*. "I have always longed for straight hair, for instance."

"I want bright blue eyes like yours."

"You do? I think your brown ones are pretty."

"Junior said your eyes are really blue. And that he thinks they're pretty."

Feeling her cheeks heat, Miriam sputtered a reply. "My goodness. That was sweet of him to say."

"He talks about you a lot, Miriam. I think he likes you."

Miriam scoffed. Junior's little sister had no idea how he really felt. "We . . . We are friends."

Kaylene studied her for a moment, then put her finger on the next paragraph and slowly read. Each word was sounded out with effort, but the pace was far quicker than it had been when they'd begun.

Miriam practically held her breath as Kaylene struggled but otherwise kept silent. She'd learned that being patient was a valuable thing with Kaylene. If she felt she had time to try her best, she read much more fluidly.

At last Kaylene finished the long paragraph. When she finished, she beamed. "I did it!"

"Indeed you did, dear. Good job! You know what, Kaylene? I think your reading is getting better every day we're together."

"Do you really think so?" Kaylene's voice sounded doubtful, but proud, too.

Miriam nodded, maybe even a bit too exuberantly. But she was as pleased as punch about her little student's progress. And, she realized, her efforts as a reading tutor. She'd been full of doubts about herself, but from the very first, she'd been able to sense what Kaylene truly needed . . . which was help believing in herself.

As Kaylene's confidence grew, Miriam thought that her reading ability and comprehension were improving, too.

Miriam chuckled. "I think we make a *gut* team, you and I."

Kaylene laughed. "You're funny, Miriam. And so nice, too."

"I think the same thing about you," she said, just as she saw Junior approach out of the corner of her eye. "But now I think it's time we said good-bye for the day. Your brother Junior has arrived. Once again he's here, right on time."

Kaylene swiveled her body and gave a little wave. "Hi, Junior."

After glancing at them for a good long minute, Junior knelt down on the blanket. "Hi, there, sister. How is the reading lesson going today?"

"Miriam says I'm doing better. And that you always get here right on time."

Junior winked. "Some of us hate being late," he teased.

Miriam laughed. "I guess Kaylene's told you that I'm always about five minutes tardy?"

"Uh-huh. So . . . things are going good with the reading today?"

"Really good. I have to say that we've made *wonderful-gut* progress since we've begun these lessons. Kaylene is going to be able to read just about everything before we know it."

"That's good news. Right, Kay?"

Little Kaylene nodded. "When are we going to meet again?"

"It can't be next Tuesday," Miriam said reluctantly. "One of the ladies I work with is going on vacation so I am picking up her hours. But I can help you next Wednesday or Thursday."

Kaylene pulled on Junior's shirt. "Junior, did you ask her yet?"

"Oops, I had almost forgotten."

Miriam looked from one to the other. "Ask me what?" Junior looked a little sheepish. "Actually, Kaylene and I have been talking and we're hoping that you could come out to the farm next time you tutor her."

"You want me to come to your house?"

"*Jah*. It's not too much farther than the school-house. See, if you come over, then Kaylene can simply go home right after school."

"Then everyone won't know I'm stayin' after to learn to read better," Kaylene filled in.

Miriam had never thought about that. "I bet that can be hard, huh? Everyone knowing that you need help."

"Some kids tease me," Kaylene said quietly. "But it would be real fun if you came over, too. Would you come over, Miriam? Please?"

"Of course I will." She thought quickly. "How about this? I'll stop by around four o'clock next Thursday. That way you'll have had some time to get home and have a snack."

Kaylene was all smiles. "Okay."

"After you two read, you'll have to stay with us for supper," Junior said.

"That isn't necessary."

"Sure it is. I don't want you to go home without supper. Plus, I know everyone is going to want you to stay. Right, Kaylene?"

"Oh, *jah*. Then you can even see Neil's baby goat."

Despite her vow to stay away from Junior, Miriam's heart was pulled in by the little girl. "Okay. I'll see you all next Thursday at your house at four."

Junior smiled. "Great. Listen, Kay, help Miriam clean up. I've got to go check in with Mary Kate real fast."

Miriam tried to avert her gaze, busying herself with folding up the blanket. But she could feel Junior's eyes on her. She turned around. "Did you need something?"

Junior looked sheepish. "Well, I just thought I'd let you know that, see, um, Mary Kate and I are finally going out to supper."

It took a lot of effort, but she did her best to remain aloof. She felt his gaze drift across her face, as if he were searching for signs of her feelings.

"That's great. I hope you both have a good time," she murmured.

"*Danke*. I'm sure we will."

When he walked away, Kaylene wrinkled her nose. "I wish he wasn't going to take my teacher out to supper."

Miriam smiled sympathetically at the girl but didn't say a word.

After all, she couldn't help it, but she was thinking the very same thing.

Chapter Twenty-two ƒ

Their appearance together at the Sugarcreek Inn caused quite a stir. More than one man gave him a wink as he helped Mary Kate down from the buggy and escorted her through the parking lot.

Junior pretended he couldn't care less about all the curious glances cast their way, but it was obvious that Mary Kate didn't like the attention.

Once again his protective instincts came to life and he gently took her arm. "No one means any harm," he murmured as they walked through the front door. "Folks just like to talk, you know."

"I know." But she still seemed more than a little perturbed.

He tried to pat her arm reassuringly. "Don't forget, we're only here as friends. I don't expect anything more."

"I'm glad about that. Otherwise I would have never said yes." Her curt reply caught him up short. As usual.

Jana Kent seated them at a booth in the back. When they got settled, he pulled out his menu, but didn't look at it. Instead, he looked at Mary Kate, half waiting to do what most women he knew did . . . comment on their booth or the menu or, well, something.

But Mary Kate merely studied her menu.

Junior had eaten at the Inn so many times over the years that he practically had the whole menu memorized.

The truth was that he would have been glad to eat at any place other than the Sugarcreek Inn. The restaurant was filled with things that reminded him of Miriam. Luckily, she didn't appear to be working tonight. But he still couldn't help but be reminded of his last awkward meal here, where he'd put his foot in his mouth and ruined their friendship.

When Christina Kempf came to take their order, he found himself smiling at her a little too brightly. "Hi, Christina, how are you today?"

"I'm *gut*, Junior." She smiled. "I saw Kaylene the other day. She was over at our *haus*, playing with my little sister, Leanna."

"She told me." Remembering how his sister had talked about the relationship between Mr. and Mrs. Kempf, he added, "Kaylene always has a nice time when she's at your *haus*."

"She's a nice little girl."

Christina looked like she was about to add something more, but when she glanced Mary Kate's way, her behavior became much more businesslike. "Do you two know what you'd like to eat? Or do you want to hear about the specials?"

Before he had a chance to say he would, Mary Kate spoke up.

"Do you have soup?"

"We do. We have three kinds tonight. Split pea and ham, vegetable, and tortilla."

"I've never heard of tortilla soup. What's that?"

"It's a Mexican soup," Christina explained. "It's chicken soup with chilis and cheese. And tortilla chips, too. It's really *gut*." Before they could ask who in the world had started making Mexican soup, she added, "Mrs. Kent's friend Pippa gave her the recipe. Marla in the kitchen decided to try it out tonight. It's real good."

Mary Katherine smiled. "I'll have a bowl of that and the salad bar."

"I'll have the same," Junior said. When Christina left, he grinned at Mary Katherine. "Isn't it funny how even a new soup can shake things up in here?"

"*Jah.*"

"I've often thought that the Lord's timing is perfect."

"How so?"

"Well, there have been different times in my life when He's brought forth a great many changes. Sometimes I didn't think I wanted the changes, or that I wasn't strong enough to handle them. But without fail, He proved me wrong. It's like the Lord knew what I needed before I knew it myself. Have you ever felt like that?"

She looked uncomfortable. "I know the Lord is always looking out for me, but I can't say that I've always been grateful for everything that's happened to me. The truth is that I'd be perfectly happy to have a life where there were no surprises and where nothing ever changed."

"Are you sure about that?"

"But of course. A lifetime of everything always being the same sounds wonderful to me."

"I know you said you were in a bad relationship back in Millersburg. Do you want to talk about what happened?"

The guardedness that usually clouded their conversations was back. "Definitely not."

"Mary Kate . . ." he asked, this time a bit softer, hoping to get her to open up.

Not meeting his gaze, she stood up. "I'm going to get my salad now."

He stood up and followed her to the salad bar that lined the back wall. As they got their chilled plates and loaded them up with potato and macaroni salad, fruit ambrosia, and broccoli salad, too, Junior kept thinking about what Mary Katherine had said.

And the way she said it.

After they sat back down, he decided to ask a couple more questions. He was worried about her, and knew that holding in something upsetting never made problems go away. "Mary Kate, I'm really good at listening." He winked. "All my siblings say so."

But she didn't crack even the slightest of smiles.

He didn't think she was going to respond at first. But then she set her fork down. "Junior, this . . . this conversation we're having is exactly why I kept saying no to you. I'm not in a good place right now. I don't want to start dating again, and I really don't want to start telling you secrets in the middle of a restaurant." She pressed her hands on the table. "I don't mean to make you upset, but you really do need to start listening to me."

Junior felt his neck heat. She was right. Time and again, she'd pushed him away. But instead of respecting her wishes he simply pushed harder.

"You're right," he said. "You're exactly right. I'm sorry. I wanted to help you, but now I realize I was being presumptuous."

Mary Kate smiled tiredly. "I'm so happy to hear you say that."

"I'm sorry it took me so long to truly listen. And I promise, from now on, we'll keep our friendship easy and simple."

"Easy and simple sound really good to me, especially since I don't think I'm going to be in Sugarcreek for much longer."

He looked up from his plate. "What are you talking about?"

She drummed her fingers on the table. "I've been thinking about moving from here as soon as the school year is over."

"Out of Sugarcreek?"

"You sound like I'm talking about going to China."

In their circle, to move away from all their friends and family, away from everything they'd ever known? It was practically like going to China. It might as well have been. "But what about your job? What about the school?"

"The school board will just have to find a new teacher." She speared two noodles, lifted her fork, then with a frown, set her fork back down. "Actually, I think that might not be a bad thing."

"And why is that?"

"Well, you've seen how I've done with Kaylene. I don't think I'm a very gifted teacher. *Nee*, that isn't putting it right. I'm not a good one at all." She drew a breath, then said bluntly, "Even Miriam is a better teacher than me. Much better."

"Even Miriam," he murmured. As seemed to be the case now, every conversation he had returned to Miriam. "You've been trying your best, though. Right?"

"What? Oh, sure."

The reply sounded flippant to him. A bit forced. "You know, I never did ask. . . . How did Miriam come to be my sister's tutor?"

"Miriam volunteered. We were sitting around one day looking at magazines, and when I told her about our conversation, since Miriam loves to read so much, she volunteered to tutor Kaylene."

"She never told me that."

"Well, she wouldn't, would she? I mean, Miriam isn't the type to toot her own horn. She seems to be more the type of woman to do what is needed."

"Yeah. I guess she is that way." He cleared his throat. "So, where do you think you might go?"

"Florida." She smiled for the first time all evening.

"Where in Florida? Pinecraft?"

"Probably. It's far from here. And it's supposed to be a nice place."

These weren't new plans. She'd had them on her mind for some time. As the reality of their situations sank in, Junior felt his skin flush.

Instead of letting his head and his heart guide him, he'd been struck by a pretty face and had let his imagination run wild. He'd assumed that Mary Katherine would be happy to have him court her . . . because most women of his acquaintance had enjoyed his attentions.

He'd known he was considered a catch. So he'd naively assumed he could fix his attentions on any woman he wanted.

But now it was becoming very apparent that he had just received his just deserts. It wasn't just Mary Kate's skittishness that was the problem. She had never had any interest in him. She'd shown him all the signs, too. He'd chosen to ignore them.

But he couldn't say he was brokenhearted. Now that he was getting to know her better, he realized that he wasn't in any danger of falling in love, either.

Actually, now he couldn't wait for their date to end.

When Christina arrived with a tray holding two large bowls of steaming tortilla soup and fresh bread, he dug into it like it was his last meal.

"This is delicious," he said with more enthusiasm than a bowl of soup had ever warranted.

"It certainly is," Mary Katherine echoed. She, too, was eating the soup with gusto. Hardly stopping in between bites.

Making him realize that she was finding their time together to be just as endless as he was.

Chapter Twenty-three 〜

"Today is the day the Lord has made," Judith murmured to herself as she dipped her mop into the lemon-scented water. "Let us give thanks and be glad."

This was the fifth time she'd said the Scripture verse and she had to admit that she did feel better. And she was glad.

Their brief visit to her parents' house had been good medicine for both Ben and herself. Her family had the amazing ability to both coddle her and treat her with a casual indifference. Before she had known it, she'd taken her place at the sink next to her mother and whatever sister-in-law happened to be visiting. Just like in years past, she'd found comfort in the security of her family.

Day after day, she'd helped gather eggs and read to Maggie and weed her mother's garden. She'd laughed at her mother's need to continually try to manage everyone—and had fallen asleep next to Ben every night almost the moment her head hit the pillow.

Two days ago they'd come home, each thankful for the peace and quiet of their own house.

It was nice to be home.

Now, here it was, almost four o'clock, and

she'd had her most productive day in weeks. Soon after Ben had gone to the store, she'd made two loaves of bread and a banana cream pie. Then, she'd worked on a blanket she was crocheting for Lilly and Robert Miller's baby shower.

Thinking about Lilly had put things in perspective. Years ago, Lilly Allen and her family had moved next door to Judith's parents during a particularly dark time in Lilly's life. Only a high school student, Lilly had been pregnant and her parents had moved so she could give the baby up for adoption without any of her friends finding out.

But Lilly wasn't sure she wanted to give the baby up. Almost as soon as she'd decided to raise the baby herself, she'd had a miscarriage. Judith remembered her being just as depressed as Judith had been lately.

Months later, however, she'd met Robert and had fallen in love. They'd had many obstacles to overcome. Robert was an Amish widower who was many years older than Lilly. Lilly was English, and just out of her teens.

The list of people who thought their relationship was inappropriate had been long, indeed!

In the end, they'd chosen love over everyone else, and now Lilly was about to deliver their first baby . . . much to the delight of all their family and friends.

The Lord had proven to them all that time really did heal wounds. And that His love was infinite.

After working on the blanket for a blissful hour, Judith had decided to give the house a good cleaning. Though Ben would never say anything, she knew he would be happy to come home to a clean house.

Over and over she dipped the mop in the water, wrung it out, and glided the mop over the linoleum. She moved backward like her mother had shown her years ago, keeping her footsteps off the clean floor.

She'd just gotten to the front door and had opened it, intending to let in the fresh air—using the wet floor as a good excuse to sit on the front stoop and enjoy the sunny day—when her husband walked up the front sidewalk.

"Ben, is everything all right? You are home early."

"I'm fine. But I think I should be the one concerned. What are you doing, sitting out on the front stoop?"

"Simply taking a break from housework." Briefly, she told him all about her day and how productive she'd been.

Crouching beside her, he smiled, then carefully lifted her chin and kissed her sweetly. "You must be feeling good today."

"I am. I made you a pie, too. Banana cream."

"That deserves another kiss," he teased as he proceeded to do just that.

Judith knew she should be embarrassed to be kissing him outside in the daylight, but she wasn't. At last, the darkness that had been surrounding her days had lifted, leaving her with a new appreciation for the good things in her life. If she knew anything, it was that sweet moments like this were ones to be treasured, for sure.

"I never get tired of kissing you, Judith," he whispered, his lips brushing the nape of her neck.

She shivered at his touch. "Me, neither."

Smiling, he sat beside her on the stoop. "Guess what? I have something to show you."

Only then did she notice that he'd set a packet of papers down before he'd kissed her hello.

"What is all that about?"

"I talked to a couple of people and got some paperwork about adoption."

She swallowed. "Adoption?"

"*Jah*. About us adopting a baby," he said in an almost carefree way.

Almost as if he were discussing getting a new kitten.

And just like that, her happiness dimmed. "You talked to people about this without me?"

He nodded.

She felt completely betrayed. "Ben, how could you?"

"I did it because I thought it was the right thing to do. I didn't want you to spend hours and hours worrying about it, wondering if now was the right time."

"But we should have discussed it."

"Judith, I won't take this further until you decide if you want to."

"And if . . . ? Ben, what if I don't ever want to?"

"Then I'll do whatever you want to do. But I think sometime over the next few days you should read this information."

She loved her husband and how he ached to keep her happy. But this didn't fix anything. "Ben, I wanted a baby of our own," she said after debating whether to say anything at all. "I wanted a baby that looks like both of us."

"I know. I did, too." He gazed at her solemnly, telling her without words that he'd been hurting, too. After a moment, he said quietly, "But, Judith, I think we have to begin to think about things in a different way. Do we want to only dwell on what we can't have? Or should we consider hoping for something else? Judith, I think it's time we started thinking about the future."

His words were sweet. So sweet. And she hated to disappoint him, but she feared he was setting them up for even more pain. "You make it sound so easy."

"I don't think it is. But . . . I don't think it would

be easy for a woman to give up a baby. Or for a child to grow up without parents. Maybe, just maybe, we could make our situation into something more positive."

She heard the longing in his voice. Saw the hope in his eyes. She wanted to make him happy, she truly did. But . . . "Ben, you are a mighty *gut* person. And I love you, too. But I'm simply not sure. . . ."

"Then do me a favor and read the packet. Don't push this idea away without doing some thinking and praying first. Please, Judith."

She stared at the packet and sighed.

And then she thought of everything her husband had been through. When he was thirteen, his mother had left him and his sister. His father had taken out his hurts and helplessness on Ben—and Ben had taken all the anger so his sister wouldn't be harmed.

Two years ago, when he'd come back to Sugarcreek after his *daed* passed away, he'd returned only to try to sell the house. The only thing he'd wanted was to sell the house and move on. But then, her father had asked him to help out at the store and a series of events transpired to enable them to both share their feelings for each other.

Judith learned that he'd always fancied her. She soon admitted that she'd also felt something special for him. Little by little, Ben began to trust her enough to share his heart. She'd been so touched when he admitted that he'd forgotten that some dreams were possible. It had taken the magic of Christmas to remind him of that.

If he could come back to Sugarcreek, face his demons, and dream of a life filled with love, couldn't she try to overcome her hurts, too?

Wasn't it time for her to face the future and start looking toward the things that she could have . . . instead of the things she couldn't?

Of course it was. Ben was so good to her. She knew in her heart that there was absolutely nothing he wouldn't do for her. If all he was asking was for her to read about adoption . . . she knew she could do that.

"All right. I'll look at the papers soon."

"*Danke.*" He took her hands then. "Now that that is settled, what would you like to do?"

"I don't know."

"Since we have to stay off the floors and let them dry. . . ."

"Yes?"

"How about we lie down on the grass and look at the clouds?"

"What in the world?" she asked as he tugged her a bit and walked her to a portion of their front yard where the grass was especially thick and vibrant and soft. She was tempted. She really was. But what if someone saw? "Ben, if someone sees us they're going to wonder what we're up to."

"If they are rude enough to ask, I'll be glad to tell them that I decided it was a *wonderful-gut* day to watch the clouds." And with that, he lay right down and pulled her down with him.

She laughed as she relaxed beside him, feeling all of six years old again. "You are a strange man, Ben Knox."

"So I've been told," he said with a smile in his voice. "But look."

Finally, she stared up at the sky and gazed at the puffy white clouds hovering so far above them. The clouds looked like cotton balls, with the cotton pulled out in different ways.

They were nothing out of the ordinary, but her appreciation of them was. "Oh!" she said.

"I spy, with my little eye, a squirrel."

"A squirrel?"

Ben lifted his hand and pointed to a cloud. "Notice his fluffy tail? I think he's holding a nut."

"It looks more like a lamb to me."

"Judith. Use some imagination," he said a bit indignantly. "Anyone can imagine a cloud looking like a lamb."

"Well, it's not a squirrel."

"What is it, then?"

Judith peeled her eyes. Trying to imagine what it could be. Then she realized how happy she felt. Why, that cloud could be anything . . . just like her future could be. If she somehow found the courage to stop looking for only the things she wanted to see.

"It's . . . It's a bumblebee. A giant bumblebee," she said. "It's buzzing over our heads, looking for honey."

Ben reached for her hand and threaded his fingers through hers. "Good job, Judith," he whispered. "Good job, my love."

She smiled to herself. Knowing he was praising her for so much more than looking at clouds.

Chapter Twenty-four ƒ

"I think if I was Jo, I'd be scared to go to the big city," Kaylene declared to Miriam.

Miriam smiled at her from the other side of the blanket they'd set out on the lawn in between the Beilers' sprawling home and their barn. "I think I would've been scared, too. It's hard to do things that are new and different."

"Like learning to swim," Kaylene murmured.

"*Jah*. Or um, learning how to ride a bike."

Kaylene smiled. "Or learning how to feed the chickens. When I first started gathering eggs the hens would peck me something awful."

"I guess there are a lot of things that are scary when they're new," Miriam stated. The least of which was her visit to the Beilers' home today.

Though she knew all of Kaylene's and Junior's siblings well enough to say hello at church or if they saw each other at the store, she'd never been to their home. In some ways, she'd always been intimidated by the Beilers. Despite having lost their parents, they were a self-assured bunch. And they all happened to be personable and attractive. Nothing like the wallflower she had always been.

The light was waning on the beautiful fall day. Closing the book, Miriam stretched. "I think

233

we're done for today. Want to show me Neil's goats now?"

Kaylene scrambled to her feet. "Uh-huh."

After they folded up the quilt, Miriam set it and her tote bag next to one of the oak trees that dotted the yard. Then she followed Kaylene to a pen behind the barn.

"This is Daisy," Kaylene said as a little brown-and-white goat spied them and ambled forward. "She's my favorite."

Miriam reached down and gently petted Daisy's coat. "She's very pretty. And her coat is so soft."

Kaylene beamed. "I named her."

"I thought you might have. Daisy doesn't sound like a name your brother would have come up with."

After Kaylene showed her the beagle puppies and the chickens, they picked up Miriam's tote bag and then headed to the house. As they walked, Kaylene chattered by her side. Miriam smiled and commented appropriately, but her mind kept wandering to another member of the Beiler family. The one person who still made her insides feel like she was filled with fluttering butterflies, and probably always would—no matter how much she wished otherwise.

The moment they opened the back door, Claire burst over to meet them. "At last you two are done! Junior made us promise to give you your privacy, but it's been so hard. Beverly and I kept peeking out the window, checking to see if you were still reading together."

"We finished, then I took her to meet Daisy," Kaylene said importantly.

Claire grinned. "Ah, Daisy. She's surely got the prettiest name in town."

Kaylene tugged on Miriam's apron. "I'm gonna go up to my room for a minute. I'll be right back."

"All right, dear," Miriam said. As Kaylene wandered off, she wondered when saying something so motherly had felt so normal. She felt a little self-conscious about it, too. Looking at Claire, she murmured, "Kaylene and I have become *gut* friends."

"So she's told us." Waving a hand, she invited Miriam into the kitchen. "Would you like some hot tea? Or maybe *kaffi*?"

"Tea would be great, *danke*."

As Miriam watched Claire bustle around the kitchen, heating water in the kettle on the stove, carefully placing slices of banana bread on a serving dish, then bringing over a metal tin of tea bags, little by little, the muscles in her shoulders eased. For some reason, she'd expected the house to be noisy and chaotic. She'd imagined that Junior and several of his brothers would be asking her all kinds of questions. She'd envisioned feeling like a fish out of water.

Instead, she was here with Claire, about to enjoy a relaxing cup of tea.

Soon, however, Miriam began to get the feeling that things weren't quite as relaxed as they seemed.

"I told the boys to grill hamburgers and hot dogs for dinner so we could have a little chat before supper," Claire said after she sat down.

Miriam put the chunk of bread she'd picked up back down. "Oh?"

"Don't look so worried! I only wanted to visit with you about Junior."

If Miriam wasn't worried before, she would surely be now! "What about Junior?"

"Only that we've all noticed that you've been on his mind lately." Her smile broadened. "You come up in conversation fairly often."

Miriam didn't know what to say. "Well, we have become friends, I suppose."

"We're glad about that. I know I'm a couple years older than you, so our paths really haven't crossed a whole lot. But I am looking forward to getting to know you better."

"Me, too." Feeling like she was having a different conversation than Claire was, she went back to familiar territory. "I've enjoyed getting to know Kaylene."

"And we've all appreciated your help."

Claire's direct gaze was starting to make her a little uncomfortable. "It was nothing. She needed a little help and I had time."

Claire gazed at her a full minute, then leaned

back in her chair. "I'm making you uncomfortable, aren't I? I'm sorry. Everyone in the family says I'm too direct." She wrinkled her forehead. "I imagine they're right, too. But listen, all I wanted to tell you is that all of us think that you and Junior would make a real fine couple."

"What?"

"Oh, I know you don't need our blessing or anything. But I figured it might feel a little awkward even thinking about joining a family that has no parents, only lots and lots of nosy siblings. I hope, over time, you won't feel that way."

Feeling beyond embarrassed, Miriam cleared her throat. "I'm sorry, but I'm afraid you've gotten the wrong impression of everything between Junior and me. Junior likes Mary Kate Hershberger."

Claire shook her head. "No, I really don't think so."

"I promise, he does. He even took Mary Kate out to supper recently. He and I are nothing more than friends."

Claire looked like she was about to argue the point, but just then the door opened and the rest of the family blew in.

The kitchen went from cozy to chaotic in two seconds. The men came in with plates filled with grilled hamburgers, hot dogs, and toasted buns.

"I hope you're hungry, Miriam," Junior said as Levi opened the refrigerator door and started setting out condiments. "We've got enough here to feed a small town."

"I'll do my best," she said with a tight smile. As more food was taken out of the refrigerator, Kaylene ran into the room, and paper plates were passed around, Miriam did her best to act like she was having a *wonderful-gut* time.

But inside, she felt like crying. In her heart, she knew that she could be a great part of the family. She knew she would get along with Claire and Beverly and all of the other siblings. She knew she could act motherly to Kaylene and give her lots of hugs and help and smiles.

Jah, she would be an excellent member of the Beiler household. If she and Junior Beiler were really a couple. Instead, Junior had reserved that place of honor for Mary Kate.

She just hoped Mary Kate would eventually appreciate what a wonderful thing that was.

Chapter Twenty-five ƒ

The knock on her door was light and brisk. Thinking Miriam had stopped over again for a quick chat, Mary Kate opened the door without first glancing through the peephole.

She regretted that immediately.

"Will." She stared at him with a mixture of shock and trepidation.

"Mary Katherine." He stared at her with something that looked suspiciously like triumph in his eyes. "Are you surprised to see me?"

She couldn't speak. Couldn't seem to form a single coherent thought.

His postured stiffened, whether from her lack of response or her obvious fear, Mary Kate didn't know. After the space of a heartbeat he murmured, "You didn't think I'd come, did you?"

She had hoped he wouldn't find her. But deep down, she'd always feared he would.

Afraid to say a word, Mary Kate attempted to push the door closed. If she caught him off guard, she could slam the door, deadbolt it against him, and simply bide her time until he got tired of waiting for her to emerge.

But one of his strong arms held the door in place. Voiding her plans.

Now she had no choice but to speak to him. "Will, you need to leave. Now. You shouldn't have come."

"That's not what your parents said. They know there's something special between us, just as I do." His lips curved upward in a parody of a smile. "That's why it was so easy to find out all I could about you. You shouldn't have run. That was a mistake. I will always find you, Mary Katherine."

He'd always called her by her full name. Never, ever had he called her Mary Kate. "My parents don't speak for me."

"It's not like you have a choice. You should honor your parents. Just as you will one day honor your husband." Still his hand gripped the edge of the door, his sheer strength preventing her from pushing it closed.

"I will honor my husband. But that man will never be you."

Will's eyes narrowed.

When she'd been in Millersburg, she'd never stood up to him. Instead, she would let him talk over her or she'd pretend that he really wasn't quite as bad as she'd feared.

But when he truly couldn't take the fact that she didn't fancy him, she started to really worry. He wouldn't take no for an answer, and would lurk around, following her, never letting her move on. As his attentions started to get more and more sinister, Mary Kate had felt as if she'd had no choice but to leave.

But all she really knew now was that she didn't feel safe when he was near her—and that he seemed to enjoy her being afraid of him. It took all her willpower to pretend she wasn't affected by his sudden appearance. "Will, you shouldn't be here at my apartment. You know how people will talk, saying that two unmarried folks shouldn't be alone like we are."

"No one saw me come in. And even if someone did, it wouldn't matter. I've been in Sugarcreek a couple of weeks now. Looking and listening. Watching you. Folks have already been talking about you, Mary Katherine."

Hearing that he'd been watching her without her knowledge made her skin prickle and her hands start to shake. "You shouldn't have done that, Will. It isn't right."

But, just like always, he continued on, as if she'd never uttered a word. "To my shame, it seems that men can't help but talk about you, help but notice you. Men can't help but follow you around, try to gain your attention." His voice cracked a bit. "And you've let them."

"I haven't been with other men."

He lowered his voice. "Oh, we know that's a lie, don't we?"

Mary Kate desperately peeked through the open doorway, hoping against hope that she could formulate some kind of plan. Unfortunately, she was as alone as ever. She had the only apartment above a vacant hardware store that was up for sale.

No cars were in the alley below. No men or women walked nearby. She was as isolated as one could possibly get in Sugarcreek.

Goose bumps formed on her arms. What should she do? Let him keep talking, in the hopes that he would wear himself out and leave on his own? Or should she continue to try to force him out and then lock her doors?

Hoping the Lord would look out for her, she decided to keep talking. "I haven't let anyone do anything I would be ashamed of."

"Mary Katherine, *nee.* I've seen that Junior Beiler walk into the schoolhouse when you were all alone. I saw him eating with you at the Sugarcreek Inn. Why are you leading him on when you know that you'll always be mine?"

A cold knot formed in her stomach. "All I did was share a quick meal," she said. "There is nothing wrong with that. I mean, my goodness, we've shared many meals over the years."

"But that was different, ain't so? I mean, you were mine."

Only in his mind. The truth was that she'd never been his. All she'd ever wanted to do was have an independent life. To do what she wanted, when she wanted.

But Will had always been there, on the out-skirts of her existence, watching, judging. Promising her parents that he'd always look out for her. Promising that he'd never let her go.

She gazed at the open space beyond him, hoping and praying to see anyone who would hear her if she screamed for help.

"Will, if you don't leave, I will go to the police and tell them about you."

Amusement lit his eyes. "And what will you tell them? That a man who loves you, who has promised to always love and protect you, has come to pay you a visit?"

His voice turned darker. "And what will you say when the police visit your parents? You know they will never understand why you brought strangers into their lives. Especially since they want you to always be with me."

"My parents have nothing to do with us."

"They do. They know we're going to get married, Mary Katherine."

"I never said I would marry you." More than that, she'd done everything she possibly could to discourage him. Obviously, it hadn't been enough. At last she'd realized that the problem wasn't hers; it was his.

He still blocked the doorway. Desperate, she snaked out a hand and pulled at the handle, hoping to nudge him to one side so that she could escape.

But of course her efforts did no good. He was too strong. Her panic increased. "Will, you must leave. Right now."

"Must?" The last bit of tenderness left his gaze. All that remained was the hard stare that had haunted her dreams—and driven her to leave her home and take a job she knew she wasn't qualified for.

"I . . . I don't want anything to make things worse between us."

Reaching out, he clamped one of his hands down hard over hers and pulled her inside her apartment. With a slam, the door closed behind them. Locking her in.

"*Nee*. Mary Katherine, I'm not going to let you go. I came here to convince you to see reason. I can't keep waiting for you to make up your mind."

His grip was bruising her skin. "This isn't the way to convince me."

"Just give me a chance." His voice turning plaintive, he looked beyond her, almost as if he were talking to someone else in the room.

"I've given you a chance. Many chances."

"Not enough of one. Mary Katherine, if you listen to me, finally listen to reason, you'll finally understand. You'll understand that I'm everything you are ever going to need." He twisted her arm, causing her to cry out in pain.

"You have no choice, Mary Kate," he whispered. "I'm in control now."

Tears filled her eyes as she realized he was right. She was at his mercy. Instead of telling someone—anyone—about her fear of Will, she'd kept everything to herself. Now no one knew that she was in danger. No one knew how afraid she was to be alone with him. "Will—"

An urgent knock on the other side of the door startled them both. "Mary Kate?" the voice called out.

They both froze. Will was glaring at the door in shock.

And she? Well, she was feeling a bit of shock, too.

Junior Beiler was outside.

As the seconds passed, Mary Kate said nothing. She couldn't do much to save herself, but she could certainly prevent Junior from getting involved.

Will eyed her with a new suspicion in his gaze. "You got a new boyfriend, Mary Kate?"

"*Nee.*"

"Sure about that?"

Before she had time to answer, the knock came again, this time as three short, impatient raps.

"Mary Kate? What's going on?" Junior's voice sounded a little chiding. Then his voice turned louder. "Listen, would you go ahead and answer the door? I saw you on your landing a couple of minutes ago. I've got something I need to talk to you about. I promise, this won't take long."

Junior sounded concerned. And, truth be told, strong and capable.

Like he could handle anything, even Will.

As Will squeezed her arm and debated whether to let her answer the door, her mind began to spin all kinds of scenarios.

Maybe he'd seen Will enter her apartment. Maybe he'd seen her struggle against him. Maybe because of that, he rushed over to help her.

Maybe he'd even be able to rescue her.

If all of that was true, she ached to run to the door and let him in. But if it wasn't? She was going to be responsible for his getting hurt.

As the seconds passed, Will's face became mottled. And then he finally made his decision. "Answer him," he hissed.

Finding a reserve of courage she hadn't known she possessed, she complied. "Junior, I am here, but I'm in trouble. Please help me!"

Will's eyes widened. It was obvious he'd never imagined she would stand up to him.

And why would he have thought such a thing was possible? She'd always let him lead, always cowed under his bullying ways. But not anymore.

The doorknob rattled. Obviously, it was locked.

She reached for the doorknob and had just enough time to slide the deadbolt to the right when Will grabbed her shoulders and pushed. Losing her balance, she slammed into the wall.

She cried out.

"Mary Kate?" Junior yelled.

Will glared at her. "Don't you move," he ordered. But though his voice was firm, his eyes darted from one corner of the room to another. One of his hands started to shake as his resolve began to falter.

The doorknob rattled again before it flew open with a loud *whoosh,* banging against the wall with a hard slam as Junior rushed in. "Mary Kate! What in the world is going on?" He stopped, looked curiously at Will, then paled when he saw her on the ground.

"I'm all right." And she was. Oh, she was scared, and her shoulders burned from where his fingers bruised her. But she was going to be all right now.

"Junior, I'm so glad you're here," she said, attempting to rise to her feet. Just before Will turned and slapped her mouth hard enough for her teeth to break skin and her head to hit the floor with a hard thump. The sharp tang of blood teased her lips.

"You stay quiet, Mary Katherine!" Will screamed. "Shut up and let me handle this."

She was too frightened to do anything but pray and hope that Junior would take control of the situation.

Her eyes began to fill with tears as an incredible pain filled her head. Furious, she blinked. The last thing she wanted was for Will to cause her to shed one more tear.

"Turn around and leave," Will yelled to Junior. "Forget you were ever here."

"You'd best step aside," Junior murmured.

"Or?"

"Or you'll wish you had." When Will still tried to block him, Junior looked positively aggravated. "I work on a farm all day. I've raised four brothers. Do ya really think one cowardly bully is going to stop me?"

And with that, he grabbed Will's shirt, pushed him toward the floor, then knelt on the floor next to her. "Mary Kate? Are you all right?" His hands hovered over her, as if he wasn't sure whether to pick her up and carry her away or stay by her side.

She wasn't sure what she wanted him to do. But perhaps the best thing for everyone was for her to finally tell the truth. "I'm not all right. Will, here, forced his way in."

"And he hurt you. You're bleeding." His eyes narrowed. "And you're bruised."

"I think I hurt my head, too. But, um, I . . . I'll be okay."

"This ain't none of your concern," Will said.

"You're wrong about that," Junior said as he clambered to his feet and sighed, looking terribly put upon when Will struggled to his feet yet again. "Stay there a moment, wouldja, Mary Kate?" he muttered, just as he turned, calmly tackled Will to the floor, and then pinned him to the ground with a knee in the middle of his back.

Then, just as if he were asking for a glass of water, he said, "Mary Kate, if you could, go get me a cord or rope or something. Please."

Getting to her feet, she remembered some kitchen twine she'd bought in one of the drawers. Ignoring her throbbing head, she pulled it out and handed it to Junior. "Will this do?"

"Well enough." Still resting his knee on the middle of Will's back, Junior fingered the twine, tested it for strength, then smiled at her. "It will be just fine."

Mary Kate stood a safe distance away, torn between wanting to fall on the couch in a tired heap and actually doing something useful. "Junior, what can I do to help you?"

He glanced over his shoulder and frowned. "Why don't you sit down for a spell?"

Feeling dizzy and more than a little out of sorts, she sat and watched Junior truss up Will like a turkey.

To her amazement, Will hardly struggled. Instead, he looked more concerned about getting hurt himself.

Once Will lay immobile on the floor, Junior stood up and sat next to her. Carefully, he took her hand and squeezed. "What do you want to do with him, Mary Kate?"

It was time to stand up to Will. If Junior could so easily, surely she could finally do something besides run. Standing up straight, she ignored her swelling cheek and looked Junior in the eye. "We need the police, Junior. This Will, he's from my hometown. He's been stalking me for years."

"I haven't been stalking you. I'm your boy-friend, Mary Katherine," Will protested. "I love you. And you love me, too."

She shook her head, wincing as the pain reverberated behind her eyes. "*Nee,* I do not. I never did."

His face turned dark with rage all over again. "Shut up! Just shut up, Mary Katherine."

Junior sighed. He went to the kitchen, grabbed a dish towel, and strode to Will's line of sight. "Do ya want to be gagged, too? Because I can do that if you won't stop yelling at Mary Kate."

After a long moment, Will pressed his lips together with a fierce glare.

Junior turned to Mary Kate. "If you can make it all right, I think it would be best if you went and got the police. Of course, I'll stay here and watch over things while you're gone."

Junior was so calm, his demeanor so accepting,

the tears that she'd been trying so hard to keep at bay fell to her cheeks. Mary Kate knew she'd never felt so low in her life.

Without a doubt, all of this was her fault. She should have tried harder to get her parents to believe her when she'd told them that Will Lott was a dangerous man.

She should have told more people about Will's anger and the way he refused to ever listen to her when she told him no. She should have gone to the police and filed a report.

At the very least, she should have done something besides plan for a new place to run. "I'm so sorry, Junior," she murmured. "I didn't want to involve you in this."

"I'm glad you did, even if it wasn't on purpose. That's what friends are for. Ain't so?" When she nodded, he gestured to the door. "You'd best go. It probably ain't right to keep Will tied up like this for long."

Knowing he was right, she slowly walked to the landing, took a deep breath, and then carefully walked down the stairs one step at a time. She felt dizzy and sick to her stomach. However, she forced herself to think positively, to push away her pain. Helping Junior was what she needed to do right now. She needed to help Junior and help herself. After all, all of her worst fears had finally come true, but she'd survived. And Junior Beiler had saved her.

When she got down the stairs at long last, she took a fortifying breath and made her way down the alley to Main Street. She was close now. She knew she could make it if she just stayed strong.

Just as she turned right on Main Street, she realized that Junior had been correct after all. She had needed more friends. More friends like him.

Chapter Twenty-six ✗

When they were alone and Junior was completely sure that Will's bindings couldn't come undone, he took a seat on the couch.

Though Mary Kate had told him she'd been in a bad relationship, he'd never imagined anything like this.

Actually, he'd never spared much of a thought about men like Will Lott. He simply couldn't imagine ever harming a woman, let alone holding her hostage.

"Why are you staring at me like that?" Will asked.

"I guess I've been trying to understand you. I don't understand why you terrorized Mary Kate." He shrugged. "Actually, for the life of me, I don't understand anything you've done."

Will stared at him for a good long minute. "If you don't understand, you've never been in love."

"What you've been doing, how you've been acting? That wasn't love."

"For me, it was. I've loved Mary Katherine for all my life. For years I've been waiting for her to see me. To see how much I want her. To see how much I've always adored her. But no matter what I did or said, she didn't care." He closed his eyes, as if he were fighting off his pain. "Today I gave up waiting and hoping. I decided that I needed to do something."

"But all you did was scare her."

"That wasn't what I wanted, though. I didn't want to be like this. I wanted to be everything good to her. But Mary Katherine never wanted to listen. She never wanted to see how things really were."

Junior found Will's words so disturbing, he strode to the kitchen and poured himself a glass of water. But as he sipped, the last words that Will uttered echoed in his head.

Slowly, he set his glass down. Pressed his hands on the counter. And called himself ten kinds of a fool.

He'd come over to tell Mary Kate that he wished her well, to tell her that he'd finally understood what she'd been trying to tell him, that they could only ever be friends.

He'd even thought about asking her for advice about winning back Miriam.

But now Junior realized that all he really needed to do was finally tell Miriam what was in his heart. That at long last, he'd finally seen her for the wonderful person she was, who she'd always been.

And that he would do whatever it took to regain her trust.

"Mary Kate! Oh my goodness! You're bleeding, and your lip is swollen! Whatever is wrong?"

Mary Kate spun around to find the one face that she longed to see above all others. Miriam. Despite the pain, she felt a smile trying to form on her lips.

She grabbed her friend's arm for support. "It's too much to tell right this second. But Junior is alone with Will in my apartment and I've got to get him help as soon as possible. I'm headed to the police station right now. Can you help me?"

Miriam blinked as she obviously tried to process what Mary Kate had just said.

"But of course, Mary Kate. The police station is just up the street."

They'd walked one whole block when Miriam spied Joe Burkholder. "Joe!" she cried out. "You are an answer to my prayers!"

When he spied Mary Kate's pale face, Joe rushed over. "Mary Kate, what happened to you? Do you need some help?"

Miriam answered, her voice brisk with purpose. "I think we're all right at the moment. We're on our way to the police station. But I'm afraid Junior really does need some help. He's alone in Mary Kate's apartment with Will. Can you hurry over there?"

Joe looked completely taken aback. "Uh, I'll

go wherever you need me to go. But . . . who's Will?"

Miriam shushed him. "Don't worry about that now." After quickly giving him Mary Kate's address, she said, "Go help out Junior, wouldja? And tell him that the police will be there soon."

Joe nodded, then turned and ran back down Main Street.

"See, Mary Kate, everything is going to be all right," she soothed, just as they entered the police station. And just as Mary Kate felt like she was about to collapse.

Within minutes of their arrival, everything became a blur. The emergency medical technicians were called. Two policemen drove over to Mary Kate's apartment in a flashing patrol car, and another carefully escorted Mary Kate into a private room. Miriam stayed by her side and could barely keep her mouth from gaping open as Mary Kate told the police officer all that had happened to her in the last hour.

Several times Mary Kate had to stop to take rejuvenating breaths to gain control of herself. Her head continued to feel as if it were splitting open. The policeman offered to stop his questioning and send her to the hospital, but Mary Kate shook her head, murmured something about needing to be strong, and kept answering questions.

At the very end of her statement, Mary Kate looked at the policeman and said, "I was so scared, all I could do was just keep hoping and praying for a miracle. Then, all of the sudden, Junior showed up. He saved me, he truly did." Reaching out with a tremulous smile, Mary Kate grasped Miriam's hand. "He was the answer to my prayers!"

At last, Junior walked in the room with a big smile. "I had to see you, Mary Kate. I've been so worried."

"I've been feeling the same way about you." After a moment's hesitation, she got to her feet, walked to Junior's side, and wrapped her arms around his waist. "Junior, I'm so glad you are okay."

Junior returned her hug. "I'm fine. I trussed him up, remember? There was no way Will was going to get free without me wanting him to. And then, thanks to you and Miriam, Joe showed up, and then the police came just minutes after that." Still grinning broadly, he said, "It's been quite an adventure for me."

Feeling sick at heart, Miriam pressed herself against the wall as she continued to watch Junior console Mary Kate. He looked so brave and strong next to Mary Kate's petite frame. So caring and tender.

So very different than he'd ever been with her.

The police officer coughed. "I'm sorry to break

things up, but I've got some questions for you, Junior."

Junior sat down. "I understand."

Then the policeman turned to Miriam, his gruff expression shaking her out of her daze. "Miss, I'm afraid you're going to need to go to the waiting room or something. Mary Kate needs to go to the hospital, so I'll be sending for an ambulance."

"Oh! Oh, of course." After smiling weakly at Mary Kate, Miriam backed away. "I think I'll just be going home now. It seems Mary Kate is in good hands."

Miriam rushed through the door, turned the corner, and hurried back to her house. All she wanted to do was hide in her room and have a good cry. It was obvious that Junior and Mary Kate were finally going to be happy together. If that hug was any indication, they would probably be inseparable for the days and weeks ahead.

She should really be happy for them. And maybe this would mean Mary Kate would stay in town. She would lose another friend to marriage, while continuing to forge ahead alone.

She shook her head, trying to dislodge the thought. Just as she stepped on her front porch, her mother rushed out. "Miriam, someone just stopped by to tell me you were in the police station with Mary Kate! What in the world happened?"

Since she knew her mother wasn't going to be satisfied unless she heard the whole story, Miriam took a seat on one of the rockers and started telling her *mamm* all about Will Lott, Mary Kate's fear of him, and how Junior Beiler saved the day.

Her mother listened in fascination until Miriam came to the very end. Lines of concentration—and a good dose of confusion—formed on her brow. "Wait a minute. Why was Junior paying Mary Kate a call? He's courting you."

Miriam bit her lip, then leaned back in her chair, resigning herself to telling her mother the whole terrible truth. "Junior never liked me, Mamm. He liked Mary Kate. He was only coming over here to ask for my help."

"But that's not what you told us." She frowned. "Miriam, we thought you two were interested in each other."

"He wasn't. Not really." She knew right then and there that her mother would never have any idea just how hard that was for her to admit. "Junior and I are friends, nothing more."

Her mother slumped. "Are you sure?"

"Oh, *jah*. He doesn't like me like that, Mamm."

Her mother rocked back and forth, gazing at her, gazing at the empty street in front of them. Finally, she nodded. "Well, all right, then."

Relieved that telling the truth hadn't been a

more painful exercise, Miriam made a move to stand up.

"Not just yet, Miriam." Her mother shifted in her chair, then brightened her voice. "You know what? I think you should start going to the singings after church on Sundays."

Miriam could hardly believe what she was hearing. She'd just poured her heart out to her mother, told her how her best friend had just been held captive in her apartment . . . and this was her response?

"Mamm, I think we both know I am too old to do that."

"Sometimes there are older men and women there," her mother continued, just as if Miriam had never spoken. "Um, I've even heard that sometimes men and women around your age participate from time to time."

This was truly awful. "Mamm, if anyone is there who is my age, it's because they're there chaperoning."

"Well, you need to do something." With a bit of effort, she rocked forward in her chair, then stood up. "Miriam, let me be blunt with you. If you keep holding out hope for a man like Junior Beiler, well, you're going to be terribly disappointed. And alone for a *verra* long time. I am mighty sure that you are going to be a wonderful wife and mother. But you must give someone else a chance before it is too late."

The prediction hurt. Unfortunately, there was a lot of truth to the words, as well, as much as it pained her to admit. She got to her feet as well, and prepared for a fast exit. "Mamm, I hear what you're saying. And I thank you for your concern."

An eyebrow raised. "I'm glad you hear me. But are you going to really listen to some advice?"

"I listened, Mamm. I promise I did. But right now I'm going to head to bed. I'm really tired."

"Well, all right. Good night, dear."

As she climbed the stairs, Miriam thought about what her mother said. Maybe no-nonsense advice was exactly what she needed to hear. It didn't make her feel good, but she knew from experience that telling someone what they needed to hear instead of what they wanted to believe took a lot of courage. After gathering her nightgown and robe, she stepped into the bathroom and unpinned her dress. Removed her *kapp*. Turned on the shower.

And thought some more.

Yes, her present and her future were sure to be much better now that Junior was officially off the market.

As she stepped under the hot spray, she almost felt good again. Well, almost normal. With that in mind, she tried to think of all the eligible men in her circle. First of all, there was James and Robert, though she'd truly never liked

Robert. He was a bit lazy, and she'd never been one for that.

She thought some more and recalled that Clyde had always had nice eyes. And Mark liked to laugh. That had to count for a lot. Everyone always told her that humor was important in a marriage.

But neither of those men had ever struck her fancy, either.

And, she assumed, they'd felt the same way about her.

But did that really matter? Maybe what she needed to do was give them more of a chance.

Since, well, she was never going to have Junior Beiler.

And because there was no one around to see or hear her, she finally let herself cry. And cried some more, her tears mixing with the hot spray and sliding down the drain.

Chapter Twenty-seven ✗

The words came through a dark tunnel, reverberating and echoing . . . and then finally settling into her consciousness. "Mary Kate? Mary Kate, can you hear me?"

Her head hurt so terribly, she opened her eyes with the greatest reluctance. Peering at the two faces leaning next to her, she felt a mixture of surprise and sweet relief. "Mamm? Daed? When did you get here?"

"A policeman came to our house and told us what happened. Then he offered to drive us here to the hospital to see you." Her mother's bottom lip trembled as she reached out to her. "Oh, Mary Kate. I am so sorry."

"We had no idea Will was so dangerous," her father added. "Now that we've heard the whole story, I feel awful. I should have believed you when you said he wouldn't give up on you. I should have listened when you said you were afraid. I hope you will forgive us one day."

"Daed, there is nothing to forgive. He fooled just about everyone. And even though I was afraid he might hurt me, even I never imagined he would break into my apartment and try to hold me hostage."

"How are you?" her mother asked. "Are you

in a lot of pain? The doctors say you have a concussion."

"You have stitches, too," her father added. "Four of them on the inside of your mouth!"

"I thought I had a pretty bad headache," she joked. "So . . . what happened to Will?"

"Oh, he's still at the police station," her father said with a grim look. "While one policeman came to our door, another two went to his parents'. I imagine they are with him right now. And probably feeling as shocked and shamed as we are."

"So it's all over." Mary Kate could hardly believe it.

"It is all over. You are safe and Will is in jail."

"And we heard all about how brave that Junior Beiler was, tying up Will until the police could arrive."

"He really was my hero. But so was Miriam. She helped me get to the police station. Oh, and she saw her friend Joe and asked him to go help Junior. If Miriam hadn't been there, why I don't know if I would have been able to get to the police station. She is such a *gut* friend."

Her parents exchanged glances. "No one said a word about her. I guess we owe her our thanks, too."

Mary Kate struggled to sit up. "Maybe we should call her or something? Or ask someone to stop by her house to tell her thank you?"

"We can thank her in a little while," her father soothed. "Now, please try to relax. You won't have to worry about Will Lott ever again. Between the police and Will's parents and us, we're all going to make sure of it."

Having her parents at her side, the knowledge that Will would never stalk her again, that she would never have to fear seeing him again, she felt brand new.

Almost.

Her parents exchanged glances. "The hospital is going to keep you overnight for observation. We're going to let the policeman take us back to your apartment. We'll spend the night there, then come back in the morning. Okay?"

"Okay," she said with a weak smile. She was glad to see them but grateful that they weren't planning to sit by her side much longer. Conversation hurt. "That's a *gut* idea. *Danke*."

After both parents gently patted her hand, they left the room. Finally, in the silence of the room, she gazed at the pale blue walls, the silent television mounted on the wall. The IV attached to her arm.

Little by little, the sharp pounding in her head eased and her vision cleared. The muscles in her back and shoulders relaxed.

And she found herself facing a curious sensation. It took her a moment to recognize it.

Then she realized it was something she'd

almost forgotten. She was at peace. At long last, she could relax and rest.

She'd read the paperwork and had made her decision. Feeling a new spring in her step, Judith walked to the store and smiled as she saw her father and Anson helping two ladies carry a large number of bags and boxes to their car.

Anson rolled his eyes as he walked by. Being eleven.

Then she saw Ben just about the same time he noticed her.

"Judith, what brings you here?"

"I wanted to show you something." Reaching into her tote bag, she pulled out the paperwork and handed it to him.

Ben took the packet and flipped through a couple of the pages. "You filled them out."

"Yep. There's a few questions you're going to have to answer, but for the most part the packet is complete."

He grinned as he wrapped an arm around her waist. "We'll finish it up tonight and then mail it out."

"I'm excited."

"Oh, Judith, I am, too," he said, just as her father and brother walked back in.

"You two are all smiles," her father said with a happy look. "What has brought this on?"

Ben didn't answer. Instead, he looked at her.

Allowing her to make the choice about whether or not to share their news.

Part of her didn't want to let anyone know what they were doing. If they weren't able to adopt a baby she knew she was going to be devastated all over again.

But then she realized that the pain wasn't going to be any easier to bear by herself than with all her family knowing, too. More important, she wanted them to be involved. They loved her and she loved them.

"Ben and I are going to try to adopt a baby," she announced. "This is the packet we had to fill out."

Her father blinked, then smiled. "I am glad."

"Me, too," Anson said.

Ben raised his brows. "You, too?"

"*Jah*. You two are going to be *wonderful-gut* parents," he said in a way that sounded far beyond his years. "Especially to someone who needs parents."

Judith looked at her brother sharply. For as long as she'd known him, her little brother had been squirrely and rambunctious. Willful and a tiny bit spoiled. Now he was restless and constantly hungry.

But never had she known him to sound so sincere. "Thank you, Anson."

He smiled, then turned to their father. "Can I get something to eat, Daed? I'm starving."

"I believe your mother packed your lunch and it's in the cooler. You better go eat so she doesn't get her feelings hurt."

When Anson trotted off to the back storage room, her father murmured, "Anson brings enough food every day to feed all the *kinner* at the schoolhouse. It's an amazing thing, to watch him consume it all."

"What did he bring today?" Ben asked.

"His *mamm* made fried chicken. Anson brought four pieces."

"Think he might give a piece up?"

Her father grinned. "You could maybe arm-wrestle him for it. At the moment you are still quite a bit bigger than him."

"See you tonight, Judith," Ben called out as he strode toward the storage room.

Folding his arms over his chest, her father grinned. "Some things never change, eh?"

Judith chuckled. Finally, she felt bright of heart. Like she had hope for her future. At long last.

Chapter Twenty-eight ✗

The first of October dawned bright and crisp, a fitting way to celebrate the fall, Miriam thought. And a fitting way to begin her new life.

She looked down at her tennis shoes and grimaced. She'd bought the fancy walking shoes almost two years ago on a day when she'd been feeling particularly fat and out of shape. But after wearing them only twice, she'd gotten frustrated with herself and slipped them back into the box.

And then she'd carefully placed the box under her bed, out of sight. And had gone to the kitchen and made a fresh batch of brownies.

But today was a new day, and she was determined to slowly but surely become a new Miriam. From this day forward, she was going to eat less and walk more. And most important, she was going to forget about Junior Beiler and concentrate on other men.

She was also going to concentrate on making herself happy.

That was a goal that was long overdue.

With that in mind, and the idea of the number on their bathroom scale being much smaller, she picked up her pace. And when the memory flashed in her head of Mary Kate and Junior hugging? She walked a little faster.

"Miriam? Hey, Miriam!" a voice called out. "Slow down for a second, will ya?"

She didn't need to look over her shoulder to know who had yelled her name. But it definitely took everything she had to slow down enough for Junior to walk to her side.

When he got there, he smiled at her in a bemused way. "What are you doing? I went by your house, but your *mamm* said you were out for a walk."

"There's nothing wrong with walking," she said primly.

"I agree. But I thought you would have been taking it easy today."

"Oh?" She strived to be completely nonchalant.

"Oh, yes," he teased. "I know you didn't get hurt like Mary Kate did, but rushing her to the police station had to be mighty scary."

Their pace slowed until they were almost strolling. "It wasn't anything. You were the one who saved the day, Junior."

"All I did was tie a cowardly bully up with some kitchen twine." He laughed. "And I have to thank my brothers for that. We didn't hogtie each other, but we've definitely wrestled each other to the ground a time or two. And it wasn't like that Will Lott was much of a problem anyways. He's used to fighting helpless women like Mary Kate, not full-grown men."

His second mention of Mary Kate enabled her

to be brave. "So, um, I hope you and she will be happy together."

He stopped. "What are you talking about?"

She stopped next to him, though she really didn't want to dwell on his happy love life. "I heard what you told each other. I saw your hug."

"Miriam, I think you misunderstood. I was worried Will had seriously injured her! And he did. She stayed in the hospital last night." Eyeing her, he murmured, "But I wasn't at Mary Kate's apartment courting. I went over there to thank her for being so honest with me. She kept saying that we needed to be just friends and she was exactly right."

"Oh?"

"Oh, yes," he said with a smile. "I mean, after all, why would I want Mary Katherine Hershberger when I could have Miriam Zehr?"

Miriam stopped in her tracks. Was this his idea of a joke? First he made comments about her looks to his siblings, and now this? She turned on her heel and headed back home.

"Miriam, what in the world are you doing?" Junior called out.

She picked up her pace. "I'm going home." When it was obvious he was following her, she began to jog.

"But we're not done talking yet," he said between gasps of air. "Don't you want to talk about what I just said?"

As a matter of fact, she did not. Okay, maybe she did, if there was any chance he was being serious. But not on the street. Not with other people around them, watching and listening. "If you want to talk, you'll have to come to my *haus*."

"All right. But please, slow down, wouldja? You might be used to running around 'cause you're always late, but I'm sure not."

Amazed that she could still smile, she slowed her pace. A bit. "If you come over, my parents are going to think you're courting," she warned.

"*Gut*. Because that's what I'm doing. Well, that's what I'm going to do if you ever let me. Instead of attempting to run by your side."

She slowed. Could he be serious? Could he really have changed his mind?

But as she turned to actually look in his eyes, she didn't see the twinkle of a joke, but a sincere concern. A look of tenderness that she'd never seen before.

Afraid to give him yet another chance in her already bruised heart, she continued walking back to her house, to her backyard, where Junior finally collapsed in one of the lawn chairs. "I'm exhausted, Miriam. Why were you out running, anyway?"

"I wasn't running until you showed up."

He waved a hand, motioning her to continue.

"Um, I was out walking because I started a new exercise program."

He leaned his neck back, gazing at her through half-closed lids. "And why are you doing that?"

"Because I need to lose some weight, of course."

"Miriam, you do what you want. But I think you look just fine."

She didn't want to say it . . . but she couldn't seem to help herself. "You do?"

He looked incredulous. "I've never thought you were overweight, Miriam. Actually, at the moment, I can't seem to take my eyes off of you."

Taken aback, she turned away from him. She walked to the swinging bench, pushed it slightly, and watched it rock back and forth in the morning sun. Gratefully, she sat on the bench and took a deep breath. Forced herself to concentrate on the chirping of the birds and the cool breeze caress-ing her skin. And not on the fact that Junior Beiler had tagged her during her walk, persuaded her to take him home, and was now watching her swing from one of her parents' favorite lawn chairs.

"Miriam, you ready to talk yet?" he asked.

"I suppose," she ventured. Still unable to believe that she and Junior were actually having such a conversation.

Just as Junior stood up, her parents opened the back door and joined them, standing side by side like twin toy soldiers. Whether they were afraid he was going to leave or stay, she didn't know.

After looking at them warily, her mother cleared her throat. "Miriam, is everything okay?"

"Everything is just fine, Mamm."

"Are you sure?" her *daed* asked, his voice a little gruff with worry.

"I'm sure, Daed. Everything is just fine."

Her mother brightened. "Oh! Well, in that case, why don't you offer Junior something to eat, dear?"

Her eyes never leaving his, she asked, "Junior, are you hungry? May I offer you something to eat?"

He gave her a smile. "*Nee. Danke.*"

Her parents gazed at her, at Junior, and then looked at each other. Finally, her mother spoke in an overly bright voice. "Miriam, ah, I think your *daed* and I are going to go back inside."

"*Jah,*" her father said in the most stilted way ever. "Um, just let us know if you need anything."

"I will."

"Well then." Her mother paused for a moment, just like she was trying hard to think of something to say, then finally pulled at her father's sleeve and went inside.

Still looking at her intently, Junior walked to her side and sat on the porch swing. She scooted a bit to make room for him, but there was no way to escape the feel of his body right next to hers.

Right away, she was struck by just how big a man he was. And how the sun glinted on the fine blond hairs on his forearms.

And how fresh and clean he smelled. Like hay and sunshine and everything good in the world. For all her pining, she'd never been so close to him before. It certainly didn't help lessen her attraction.

"So," he said. "I came over this morning so we could talk." Turning his head, he said, "How are you? Really?"

"You know what? I'm fine. I'm thankful that Mary Kate's troubles are hopefully behind her. That is an answer to prayer, for sure. How are you?"

"Honestly? I think it's going to take a mighty long time to recover from yesterday's excitement." Then, much to her surprise, he reached out and wrapped an arm around her shoulders, pulling her closer to him. "When I saw Will slap Mary Kate in the face and then watched her fall to the ground, I was shocked. And scared."

"I bet you were." She tried to pull away, but he only took her hand with the one not wrapped around her shoulders. Now she was completely encircled in his arms.

"Miriam, I'm only telling you about Mary Kate so you'll understand what I'm trying to say to you."

"Which is?"

"It's like this. For much of my life, I think I just accepted that you'd be there, in the background. I took you for granted. Then, there I went, asking you to help me gain Mary Kate's attention, when it turned out that she wasn't even interested in me. Later, when it was apparent that we had so much in common, I still kept you at an arm's distance."

He swallowed and for the first time, looked away. "I don't know why. Maybe it had to do with my parents passing away so young? Or all the responsibility I felt, looking after my siblings? But I had been certain that falling in love would feel different."

"How did you think it would feel?"

"Like a sledgehammer. Or a lightning bolt." He grimaced. "You pick the cliché. The love I feel for my family is so strong, so unquestionable, I thought falling in love in a romantic way would feel the same. I thought there would be no doubts."

"I suppose most everyone feels that way," she allowed.

His voice lowered, turned almost hoarse. "I've learned something, though. I learned that I hadn't been recognizing the signs. I'd been searching for something that I would have seen clearly . . . if I'd only thought to open my eyes."

Before she could say a word, he continued, "Over the last few weeks, I kept seeing all the signs that you were right for me. My sister loves you, my family thinks you're perfect for me."

"And you?"

"Well, the more time I spent with Mary Kate, the more I kept thinking about you. How easy our conversations were. How much you fit into my life. When I spoke out of turn at the restaurant and you were so angry at me—rightfully so—the thought that I'd lost our friendship for good devastated me. And all I could think about was how I could win it back. Then . . . I realized how important you were to me when I was sitting in Mary Kate's living room with that blasted Will. All of a sudden, all the strong feelings I'd been pushing aside and trying to ignore hit me like that lightning bolt I'd been waiting for! I realized that I'd been a fool, waiting for the perfect time to fall in love. But of course, then it was almost too late."

Gazing at her, he said, "I was so scared, Miriam. I was so afraid I had lost you before I had even taken the chance to tell you how much I cared for you."

Miriam cleared her throat. Though Junior had just said many pretty things, he hadn't exactly come right out and said he loved her. Or that he no longer had any feelings for Mary Kate. "I don't know what to say."

Still looking at her directly, he said, "Mary Kate's parents stopped by my house early this morning to thank me for my help. They're taking her back to Millersburg. I think she's decided she needs to spend some time living instead of running."

"I think that is a *gut* idea," Miriam replied. "I have a feeling she never was able to show us who she really was the whole time she was here."

She shivered. "When I think about her burdens that she tried so hard to keep secret? It makes my head spin. She is a brave woman."

"She sure is."

Now it was time for her to be brave, too. "Junior, do you still have any feelings for her?"

"Nope. You are the only one I've been thinking about for days. You are the person I want to be around the rest of my life."

Miriam closed her eyes. These were the words she had always dreamt of hearing. Could it be possible they were really coming out of Junior's mouth? She brushed away a tear, and turned toward him again. "You sound so sure."

"It took me a while, but I promise, I've never been more sure about anything."

The brush of his thumb over her knuckles reminded her that he was still holding her hand.

And now, as the silence stretched between them, she felt something new settle comfortably between them. It wasn't friendship, or the strain of tension that hovered in the air.

No, it was something new. Something fresh. Recognizable but a little strange.

After a few seconds, she recognized it for what it was: tenderness.

"Miriam, I need to tell you something."

"Yes?"

"Last night I finally was able to put into words what I was feeling. Love. I've fallen in love with you."

Love? "Are you sure?"

"More than sure." He shifted a bit, then stood up so he was looking down at her. His voice turned like the Junior Beiler she'd known for most of her life. Confident. Assured. "So, it occurred to me that there was only one thing to do about that."

"What is that?"

"We need to be together."

She felt her lips curve up. "That is what you've decided?"

"I don't want to let you go, Miriam."

His words were so sweet, she felt tears prick her eyes again. But she needed to be sure that he was certain.

"You've always had a special place in my heart, Junior. But I don't want to be an afterthought. Or something that's 'good enough.' A substitute for what you couldn't have."

"Yesterday, when everything happened with Mary Kate? While of course I was concerned for her safety, I realized that you are the most important thing in the world to me. Let me spend

279

the rest of my life making you believe that. Proving that to you."

He took both her hands in his.

"I'm more sure about this than most anything else in my life. Miriam, you don't need to answer right now, but please think about it."

"What are you asking?"

"For you."

While she stared at him in wonder, he leaned forward, his gaze earnest and pure. "Say you'll let me court you. Let me take you on walks and rides and out to meals and whatever else we can think of. Please, let me be yours. Let me know that there's a chance we could marry one day. Let me hope that one day you'll forgive me for being so stupid. Let me love you. Miriam, give me hope."

She almost laughed. All her life, she'd hugged her hopes close to her chest, at first not wanting others to see how much she dreamed about good things happening.

Later, she kept her hopes hidden because she'd feared that others would see and make fun.

But here Junior Beiler was doing the one thing she'd always known she was terribly good at: dreaming of a future. Dreaming of happiness. Dreaming of love. Dreaming of things people said were too much to hope for.

All her life, people had said she should be satisfied with what she had. That she didn't need more. She didn't need a man like Junior. She didn't need a marriage full of romance and love.

But still, she had yearned. And, secretly, she'd continued to hope for more.

"Miriam? What do you think? Do you think one day you might be able to trust me? To trust us? Do you think one day you could love me back?" Junior's voice was strained. He was worried. He truly thought she might turn him down!

"You're asking if I might be able to love you, Junior Beiler?"

"Well, yes." His cheeks were flushed with embarrassment.

A different woman might have remembered a lifetime of longing. Perhaps that woman might have even wanted to make this man learn a bit of patience.

But time had shown her that it was impossible to be anything other than herself.

"*Jah*," she said, in what had to be the biggest understatement of her entire life. "*Jah*, Junior. I do think I could love you. And that I could trust us."

And when he looked at her, happiness lighting his eyes, she smiled right back at him.

And knew that at last, she had everything she'd ever wanted.

Epilogue ✎

So, it seemed the whole family was now inter-ested in *Little Women*. For the last two nights, they'd all gathered in the family room for story time.

"Come on, Miriam and Kaylene," Randall called out from his position on the couch next to Micah. "Don't leave us hanging."

Miriam crossed her legs from her position on the floor next to Kaylene and glared at Randall. "You're being awfully bossy all of a sudden."

"I've got reasons. Amy's happy with Laurie, Meg has babies, Beth is in heaven. But we've got to know what happens with Jo." He waved his hands in a forward motion. "Start reading."

Miriam leaned close to Kaylene. "What do you think we should do? Randall isn't being very polite."

Kaylene scooted up on her knees as she half giggled, half whispered in Miriam's ear. "I think you should read us the very end of it, Miriam."

"Are you sure?"

"She's sure," Joe called out as he grabbed a handful of popcorn before passing the bowl to Claire. Joe had finally asked Beverly to marry him so he was a constant fixture in the house.

Which meant, of course, that he got swept away by the girls' story, too.

"All right, I will. As long as you boys stop commenting after every paragraph."

"Not all of us have been commenting," Levi said with a glare at his older brothers. "Some of us actually know how to listen to a story."

Randall tossed a piece of popcorn at him. "You only know because you just got out of school. You're still just a boy."

Levi glared. "I am not. I'm practically a man."

Randall grinned wickedly. "Oh, really, Levi? What, exactly, have you been—"

"Stop egging him on, Randall," Junior interrupted before turning to Miriam. "You can start now. I promise, we'll all stay quiet."

"Well, if you're sure. . . ."

"We're sure," Randall said. "Go ahead. Please."

Hiding a smile, Miriam cleared her throat and read the last chapter.

Thirty minutes later, the book was done. She closed it with a satisfied feeling. To her amusement, everyone who was gathered around started clapping.

"That was a *gut* book," Kaylene whispered in Miriam's ear.

"And you even read much of it, Chipmunk."

Pride shone brightly in her eyes. "I did, didn't I?" She hugged Miriam and then ran to the kitchen, where Claire was serving up generous slices of pumpkin pie.

With a creak and a small groan, Miriam climbed to her feet, then smiled when Junior came forward to lend a hand.

"Thank you," he whispered.

"For what?"

"For doing something amazing."

"Junior, I didn't do anything. All I did was read a book."

"No, you did more than that. You made our little family complete. You made it seem like we weren't missing part of ourselves anymore."

She shook her head. "This was already a wonderful family. But I'm glad I'm a part of it now."

"Are you sure you don't mind being plain old Miriam Beiler and not working anymore?"

"I love being Miriam Beiler."

He still looked concerned. "You're not going to miss baking pies at the Sugarcreek Inn?"

"Believe me, I'd rather make pies for you than a dozen people at the Inn. This is where I belong."

After peeking to make sure everyone else was occupied, he folded her into his arms and gathered her close. "For sure and for certain, Miriam. For now and for always, this is where you belong."

"Forever," she whispered, as she lifted her chin for his kiss. And his love. Forever and ever.

Meet Shelley Shepard Gray ✓

I grew up in Houston, Texas, went to Colorado for college, and after living in Arizona, Dallas, and Denver, we moved to southern Ohio about ten years ago.

I've always thought of myself as a very hard worker, but not "great" at anything. I've obtained a bachelor's and master's degree . . . but I never was a gifted student. I took years of ballet and dance, but I never was anywhere near the star of any recital. I love to cook, but I'm certainly not close to being gourmet . . . and, finally, I love to write books, but I've certainly read far better authors.

Maybe you are a little bit like me. I've been married for almost twenty years and have raised two kids. I try to exercise but really should put on my tennis shoes a whole lot more. I'm not a great housekeeper, I hate to drive in the snow, and I don't think I've ever won a Monopoly game. However, I am the best wife and mother I know how to be.

Isn't it wonderful to know that in God's eyes that is okay? That from His point of view, we are all exceptional? I treasure that knowledge and am always so thankful for my faith. His faith in me makes me stand a little straighter, smile a little bit more, and be so very grateful for every gift He's given me.

I started writing about the Amish because their way of life appealed to me. I wanted to write stories about regular, likeable people in extraordinary situations—and who just happened to be Amish.

Getting the opportunity to write inspirational novels is truly gratifying. With every book, I feel my faith grows stronger. And that makes me feel very special indeed. ✗

Letter from the Author ✗

Dear Reader,

Have you ever returned to a place you hadn't visited in a long time? I did when I went back to Houston a few years ago. It had been a long time since I'd lived there— almost twenty years! To my surprise, as we drove around the city with my brother, looking at old schools, old houses, stopping at restaurants that I used to love . . . it all felt a little bit strange.

Truthfully, my high school didn't seem as big as I remembered. Our street didn't seem as endless. Even those po-boys that I used to crave didn't taste quite as good as I recalled. And it was hot. I mean, really hot. *Houston-hot.* And big! Houston is a really big city with tons of traffic and crazy freeways. Had I really used to drive on the Katy Freeway all the time? Had I ever really been used to all that heat and humidity?

Suddenly, I felt like I was very far from the confident city girl I once was. Actually, I started feeling like the person I had become—a middle-aged woman living in a small Midwestern town. To be honest, I was a bit taken aback by the whole experience.

Then I saw my girlfriends from high school

and realized that they, too, had gotten older. But yet, before we knew it, we were sipping iced tea out of Mason jars and laughing about our days on the high school drill team. All of a sudden, twenty years didn't seem like that much time at all.

I thought about my trip back to Houston a lot while I was writing *Hopeful*. I loved returning to the setting of my Seasons of Sugarcreek books and revisiting characters who still had stories to tell. It's been a pleasure to Return to Sugarcreek and to write a novel focusing on multiple charac-ters' hopes and blessings.

I sincerely hope you enjoyed Miriam's story in *Hopeful*, my twentieth book for Avon Inspire! There's lots more to come with these characters in the rest of the series. I hope you'll join me for another book very soon!

With my thanks,
and continued blessings to you,
Shelley Shepard Gray ✎

Shelley Shepard Gray
10663 Loveland, Madeira Rd. #167,
Loveland, OH 45140

Questions for Discussion ✦

1. In the book, Miriam Zehr goes from trying to please everyone but never quite succeeding to learning to be happy with herself. Have you ever experienced any of the doubts that Miriam does? If so, how did you overcome them?

2. Junior Beiler was all about responsibility. He was a great brother to his siblings, but not always the greatest friend to Miriam. Which parts of his character did you admire? Was there anything that you didn't?

3. Did you connect with any of the other seven Beiler siblings? Who would you like to learn more about?

4. As a writer, I struggled a lot with Mary Kate Hershberger's character. I knew she was in a lot of pain, both from her past and her present situation. What did you think about her? What do you think will happen to her in the future?

5. One of the main reasons I was so happy about writing another series in Sugarcreek was the opportunity to return to the Graber family. I was especially excited to continue Ben and

Judith's story. For those of you who have read *Christmas in Sugarcreek*, how do you think their past experiences will help them on their current journey?

6. Family relationships and expectations play a big role in this book. Some offered support, others brought more pressure for the main characters. Who in your family has been your base of support? How has she or he helped you over the years?

7. Obviously, being "hopeful" was one of the main themes in the book. I did a lot of thinking about hoping for things that actually could happen, and hoping for dreams that seem almost out of reach. Is there a difference between the two? Have any of your "dreams" come true that you thought were out of your reach?

8. The Scripture verse from Job, "Having hope will give you courage," guided me in the writing of this novel. How do you think having hope can give a person courage?

9. Miriam's journey in the novel certainly reflects the wisdom of the Amish proverb that opened the book, "It is far more important to be the right person than to find the right person." How could this proverb relate to you, or to someone you love?

Fanny Kay's Chocolate Cream Pie

2½ cups milk
1 cup sugar
¼ cup cocoa
¼ cup cornstarch
Dash of salt
½ teaspoon vanilla
1 baked pie shell, cooled
Nondairy whipped topping

Bring 2 cups of milk to a boil. In a separate bowl, mix sugar, cocoa, and cornstarch together. Stir in the remaining ½ cup of milk. Stir mixture into hot milk. Bring to boil, stirring constantly. Add salt and vanilla. Remove from heat and cool. Pour into baked crust and top with whipped topping.

Reprinted with permission from *Simply Delicious Amish Cooking* by Sherry Gore (Zondervan, 2012) ✗

Glossary of Pennsylvania Dutch Words

Bamhatsich, merciful, kind
Bays, mad
Bedrohwa, sad
Boppli, baby
Daed, Dad
Danke, thank you
Ehrlichkeit, honesty
Englischer, someone who isn't Amish
Frayt, happy
Freind, friend
Gmay, church
Gut, good
Jah, yes
Kaffi, coffee
Kapp, the white covering for a woman's head
Kinner, children
Lieb, love
Mamm, Mom
Moondawk, Monday
Muddah, mother
Naerfich, nervous
Nee, no
Nohma, name
Onkle, uncle

Rumspringa, the running-around years. Time
 in a teen's life to explore the outside world.
Shool, school
Shoolahs, scholars
Tay, tea
Wunderbaar, wonderful, great
Wilkum, welcome ✗

Center Point Large Print
600 Brooks Road / PO Box 1
Thorndike ME 04986-0001 USA

(207) 568-3717

US & Canada:
1 800 929-9108
www.centerpointlargeprint.com